"You're

Dan's wide hand shot out. He seized Elly by the arm and marched her firmly toward the door.

Elly had only enough time to swipe her purse from the coffee table and grab her coat from the back of her chair before he ushered her out of the room.

"I don't know what kind of game you're playing, and I don't care. You're leaving, lady."

"But don't you want to—"

Before she could get out the rest of her sentence, she found herself standing alone in the cold ocean mist on Madge's lemon-bright porch. After the door slammed behind her, she could still feel the pressure of Dan's strong fingers on her arm and his palm on her backside. The nerve of the man. He'd thrown her out!

Then the implication of what had just happened hit her. A triumphant grin spread slowly across her lips.

She had found her missing prince!

Dear Reader,

Celebrate the rites of spring with six new passionate, powerful and provocative love stories from Silhouette Desire!

Reader favorite Anne Marie Winston's *Billionaire Bachelors: Stone*, our March MAN OF THE MONTH, is a classic marriage-of-convenience story, in which an overpowering attraction threatens a platonic arrangement. And don't miss the third title in Desire's glamorous in-line continuity DYNASTIES: THE CONNELLYS, *The Sheikh Takes a Bride* by Caroline Cross, as sparks fly between a sexy-as-sin sheikh and a feisty princess.

In *Wild About a Texan* by Jan Hudson, the heroine falls for a playboy millionaire with a dark secret. *Her Lone Star Protector* by Peggy Moreland continues the TEXAS CATTLEMAN'S CLUB: THE LAST BACHELOR series, as an unlikely love blossoms between a florist and a jaded private eye.

A night of passion produces major complications for a doctor and the social worker now carrying his child in *Dr. Destiny*, the final title in Kristi Gold's miniseries MARRYING AN M.D. And an ex-marine who discovers he's heir to a royal throne must choose between his kingdom and the woman he loves in Kathryn Jensen's *The Secret Prince*.

Kick back, relax and treat yourself to all six of these sexy new Desire romances!

Enjoy!

Joan Marlow Golan

Joan Marlow Golan
Senior Editor, Silhouette Desire

Please address questions and book requests to:
Silhouette Reader Service
U.S.: 3010 Walden Ave., P.O. Box 1325, Buffalo, NY 14269
Canadian: P.O. Box 609, Fort Erie, Ont. L2A 5X3

The Secret Prince
KATHRYN JENSEN

Silhouette®
Desire®

Published by Silhouette Books
America's Publisher of Contemporary Romance

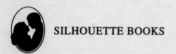 SILHOUETTE BOOKS

ISBN 0-373-76428-6

THE SECRET PRINCE

Copyright © 2002 by Kathryn Pearce

This edition published by arrangement with Harlequin Books S.A.

Visit Silhouette at www.eHarlequin.com

Printed in U.S.A.

Books by Kathryn Jensen

Silhouette Desire

I Married a Prince #1115
The Earl Takes a Bride #1282
Mail-Order Cinderella #1318
The Earl's Secret #1343
The American Earl #1347
The Secret Prince #1428

Silhouette Intimate Moments

Time and Again #685
Angel's Child #758
The Twelve-Month Marriage #797

KATHRYN JENSEN

has written many novels for young readers as well as for adults. She speed walks, works out with weights and enjoys ballroom dancing for exercise, stress reduction and pleasure. Her children are now grown. She lives in Maryland with her writing companion—Sunny, a lovable terrier-mix adopted from a shelter.

Having worked as a hospital switchboard operator, department store sales associate, bank clerk and elementary school teacher, Kathryn now splits her days between writing her own books and teaching fiction writing at two local colleges and through a correspondence course. She enjoys helping new writers get a start and speaks "at the drop of a hat" at writers' conferences, libraries and schools across the country.

One

"**Y**ou're mine, lady." Daniel Eastwood tossed his jeans on top of the sweatshirt already in the sand and fixed his dark eyes on her. "Giving me the cold shoulder won't keep me away."

She was even more beautiful this morning than she'd been the day before...or the one before that. The muscles angling across his taut stomach and lean thighs tensed, primed for action. He rolled his wide shoulders in anticipation.

Three long running strides, and he dove into the chill waves of the Atlantic. She yielded, as always, to his fierce strokes. Her cool fingers supported him, beckoned him to deeper waters, challenged him. He could feel her strength in each liquid gray-green surge. He swam exactly half a mile along the deserted beach before flip-kicking around to slice back through the icy foam, back toward where he had started, directly below the pastel bungalows of the Haven.

Dan had sustained an intimate relationship with the sea since the first day he had seen her. The school field trip to Ocean City had carried him a good three hours by bus from the grim streets of south Baltimore, a world away. Never had he forgotten the sense of awe, respect, and fascination he felt that day—a city kid, standing on that endless stretch of pale sand, so much water all in one place. Water that seemed to breathe with its own movement and the motions of living things hidden beneath it. And all that clean air hitting him in the face, filling his lungs, it made him feel strong and new inside. Although he had to return to the city with his classmates that day, he had never forgotten the ocean's beauty or wanted to live anywhere but beside her.

As soon as he was old enough, he had returned to take a summer job as a lifeguard. And each June after that, with the exception of those four he had spent with the marines, he had been drawn back to her as surely as the tide is pulled by the moon. He never lost sight of her capricious temperament, though. The unpredictable squalls. Sudden drops just off shore that hadn't been there days before. Riptides that could seize a strong swimmer, drag him out to frigid depths, and rob him of his will to ever breathe again. He loved her beauty and power, despite her faults.

As he turned his head to draw a final breath that would carry him the last four strokes of his morning regime, he glimpsed a woman standing beside his clothes, her hand held delicately above her eyes to shade them from the early-morning sun. She gave the impression of having come for him, not just someone idly watching a lone swimmer brave fifty-degree water.

"What the devil," he muttered, swallowing a mouthful of salt water in his distraction. His people knew not to disturb him at this time of day. That is, if any of them were in the office this early. Setting his feet down, he stood in chest-deep water, the sand sucking and scraping beneath the pads of his feet as he studied her.

Not a local. He would have recognized her this time of year with all the tourists gone. She was tall for a woman, maybe up to his chin, which would make her about five-nine. Her hair was russet streaked with pink-gold highlights from the dawn sky, pulled back in a prim knot at the nape of her neck. Her dark-green business suit seemed absurd beachwear. Tan leather pumps dangled from one crooked finger. Her mouth was pulled into an annoyed pout. The tiny grains of sand sifting between the threads of her pantyhose probably weren't helping her mood.

But as soon as he started up the slope out of the water, her expression changed. The water line crept teasingly down his chest, not yet revealing the presence or lack of a bathing suit. Her eyes widened with alarm. He smiled, kept on coming, and soon the upper edge of his flesh-molding Speedo showed above the white spume.

Immediately, her lips lifted in a weak smile of relief.

Dan chuckled to himself. What he would have given to have been swimming in the buff that morning, just to watch the shock in her pretty eyes.

A nippy breeze off the water hit him, and the sudden cold took his breath away. "Throw me that towel!" he called to her.

She scowled as if she hadn't at first heard him over the grating, gurgling rush of the waves against the sand. Looking around, she focused on a generous pile of terrycloth near his clothing and scooped it up. "Isn't November a little extreme for swimming in Maryland?"

"Not for me." He couldn't resist. "I'm naturally hot-blooded."

She rolled her eyes and tossed the towel at him. "Oh please—"

"Seriously. My body temperature runs two degrees above normal. Always has. I draw the line, though, at breaking through ice for my morning constitutional."

"Limits are good." Her eyes sparkled with humor.

Elly forced herself to look past the near-naked man toward the softly glowing horizon. She tried to remember the reason she was standing on a beach in the middle of winter in her stocking feet. But Dan Eastwood was very difficult to stop looking at. No male she'd ever personally met possessed a body like *that*. Wide, muscled swimmer's shoulders, a rock-hard stomach, and hips that slimmed to strong, efficient kicking levers. But she hadn't come to flirt with the owner of the Haven. Her mission was much more important than that and, she reminded herself, time was of the essence.

"You're Daniel Robert Eastwood?" she asked, risking another glance his way. God, he was gorgeous!

"I'm Eastwood. And you?"

He was drying off his beautifully muscled chest, his long, strong arms—the towel dropped lower—his *everywhere*. She looked away, tiny beads of sweat springing up beneath her hairline despite the frigid air. "I'm Elizabeth Anderson. I need to ask you a few questions, if you can spare me ten minutes."

He frowned. "If you're selling hotel supplies, you'll

need to see my business partner, Kevin Hunter. He takes care of all the ordering. His office is in the main building."

"I've already spoken with Mr. Hunter. He told me where you'd be."

"He did, did he?" She liked the way his dark eyes flashed at her, suggesting he wasn't at all displeased with his partner's decision.

With a sudden jolt, Elly realized that she had been running the tip of her tongue across her upper lip and she stopped herself. He might read the gesture as an appreciation of his near-nakedness, which of course it was. But it was crucial that she keep her mind on the business at hand. A lot of people, very important people—not the least of which was her father—were depending on her.

As Dan tugged his sweatshirt down over his head, he snuck a good peek. She looked slim and healthy, though a little on the pale side, as if her work rarely took her out into the sunshine and she didn't take much time off for outdoor recreation. Her pleated skirt was short, revealing elegant, long legs. Her breasts…hard to tell. All he could make out was a promising swell beneath the ultra-conservative suit jacket. Pity it wasn't August. She'd have been hard put not to strip down under Ocean City's blazing sun.

"Suppose we walk up to my house," he suggested. "You can tell me what this is all about."

"Why don't you get yourself dressed, Mr. Eastwood? I'll meet you back at your office."

"That's not convenient." He started walking away from her, up the sloping beach. A moment later, he heard her scurrying behind him in the sand, and he smiled to himself.

"Why isn't it convenient?" she called out.

"I have a nine o'clock. No telling how long the meeting might last. Ever heard of making appointments, Miss Anderson?"

"There isn't time. I need to speak with you right away."

Dan stopped and turned to face her. The urgency in her tone signaled trouble. "Maybe we'd better settle this right here. What's the big crisis?"

She sighed and gazed thoughtfully along the wind-swept beach then turned back to study his face with an odd intensity.

"Talk fast," he prompted. Pretty soon his fingers were going to fall off from the cold. After that, who knew what would be next.

"All right then," she snapped, giving him an irritated look. "I am a professional genealogist. I work for my father's company, and we've been hired to verify the ancestors and descendants of a gentleman, now deceased. There's a possibility you might be related to his family."

He laughed. "That's it?"

"That's it," she said. "All I need to do is ask you a few simple questions, then I'll be out of your hair." She tipped her head to observe him. "Your lips are turning blue. I suppose it's all right if we talk at your place, since it's so cold outside."

"Thank you." He stepped up onto the boardwalk that ran over a mile along the shore. Most of the structures at the far end of the driftwood-gray planks were high-rise condominiums and hotels. But here, in the older part of town, along with the arcades, snack shacks and amusement park rides, were a few of the older-style beach bungalows that had survived the ocean's violent mood swings. Four years ago when Hurricane Evelyn had swept away entire blocks of the low wooden structures, Dan had seen the opportunity he'd been waiting for. He was out of the Corps, had earned his degree in business on the GI Bill and saved up a nest egg. He was looking for an investment that would keep him close to his beloved beach.

He and his best friend Kevin put together a proposal to buy the ruined property. They raised the level of the land by bringing in tons of fill, built protective man-made dunes, then erected sturdy, smaller versions of the original bungalows—twenty-five of them in a cluster. The Haven evolved into a far more successful business than either of them had expected. Dan couldn't help feeling proud of what they'd accomplished.

But now that most of the hard work had been done, the days often ran together. The off-season was particularly lonely. After Labor Day, the tourists disappeared, including most of the dateable women. But here was pert, intriguing Elizabeth Anderson with her burnished locks, long legs, and baffling need to interrogate him. He toyed with the tempting idea of canceling his nine o'clock to spend the morning with her…if he could find a way to stretch her promised ten minutes to a few hours.

"So tell me about my mystery family." He opened the door to the first house they came to and waved her inside.

"We don't know that they *are* your family," she cautioned. "Not yet. That's why I need to talk to you."

"So shoot." He tossed the damp towel on the arm of the tan leather sofa and she followed it with a look of female disapproval for his casual housekeeping.

"What are your mother's and father's full names?"

"My mother is Margaret Jennings Eastwood. She goes by Madge. My father, I never knew. His name was Carl Eastwood. He died shortly after I was born."

She nodded, sliding a small pad of paper and pen from her purse. Elizabeth wrote a few notes. "And the date of your birth?"

He told her.

"That makes you, let's see…thirty-two?" He nodded. "Your mother's current address and phone number?" she asked smoothly.

He stopped halfway into the bedroom and turned to face her, suddenly suspicious. "Why do you need to know that?"

"I'm sure she'll be as interested as you are in your shared heritage," she said with a brilliant smile. But her eyes shifted away from his before she'd finished speaking. He wondered if she might be concealing something he should know before giving her more information.

"If you need to speak with my mother, I'll take you to her. What else do you need from *me?*"

She looked vaguely disappointed, but glanced down at her pad. Her tongue did its little lip-flick thing again. "Well…where were you born, Mr. Eastwood?"

"It's Dan. In Baltimore, Mercy Hospital."

She blinked, checked something she'd written a few pages back, then nodded. He sensed she was holding her breath as she asked the next question. "And have you always lived in Baltimore?"

"Until I graduated from high school. Then I enlisted in the Marine Corps. After that I took up permanent residence in Ocean City. We've been here ever since."

A subtle blink of her eyes told him he must have given her a piece of information she thought valuable.

That troubled him. He didn't like being kept in the dark.

"Do you have any siblings?" she continued.

"No."

"Not even half brothers or sisters by another father?"

Dan scowled, even more uneasy at the intimate turn of her questions. "What are you implying, Miss Anderson?"

"My friends call me Elly." She beamed at him—all hazel-eyed innocence. Something tightened pleasantly in his stomach, and he couldn't help smiling back despite his growing suspicion that she was setting some kind of trap for him. "It's a simple question, really," she continued. "These days, many families include step-kids, half siblings...yours, mine, and ours.... Women *are* allowed to marry more than once, you know."

"My mother never remarried," he stated quickly.

"I see."

Dan wished he could get a look at what she was writing. Her pen was in constant motion now, scratching out far more than the few words of each of his responses. The sense that his privacy was being invaded in some mystifying way that he couldn't yet understand became almost overwhelming.

"I have to change and get to that meeting," he grumbled. "Unless you're willing to be straight with me about what you're really up to, Miss Anderson, this is the end of our discussion."

Looking disheartened, she flipped the little book shut then shoved it and the pen into her shoulder bag. "I'm afraid, for the time being, anything more than what I've already told you is confidential."

"Then you'd better leave," he said gruffly. He told himself he was being an idiot, shaking off the prettiest thing that had crossed his beach in months. She looked as good indoors as she had outside in the salty air. If anything, her eyes seemed brighter, more alive than before—as if she was excited by something she had just learned.

But the meeting with his contractor really was important. And even as his libido urged him to get her phone number, his brain was warning him to distance himself from her. She was pure trouble, although what variety he hadn't as yet figured out.

"I'll let you know if I can tell you anything more," she promised coolly then stuck out her hand to shake as if determined to conclude their conversation with a professional gesture, even if it had begun under less than businesslike conditions.

"Next time, maybe you'll join me for a swim," he suggested as he opened the door for her.

She laughed. "In November? Don't hold your breath."

Too bad, he thought as he stood alone in his living room a moment later, the knob still in his hand. *I'd love to be the one to warm you up after a winter dip.*

Elly sat in her car gripping the steering wheel, trying to compose herself. Her father would be furious with her for not getting everything out of Daniel Eastwood they so desperately needed. But things had started out badly. She'd nearly keeled over when he came up out of the water—all gleaming muscles and smooth, bronzed skin. A classic vision of Neptune in his younger years, sans trident. That skimpy red Speedo hadn't left much to the imagination. Not much at all!

She felt a hot flush across her cheeks and brow and let out a yip of frustration. She wasn't usually flustered by men. In fact, she'd become pretty much immune to these feelings from choice. It was her defense against getting involved. Involvement meant intimacy, and intimacy meant...

A flash of dark memory rocked her without warning. Suddenly, she could hear and see everything as it had been that night. The high-pitched cry in the night...her father's frantic shouts into the telephone...the wretched look of helplessness on his face. And finally, her mother's unmoving body glimpsed through the half-open bedroom doorway seconds before sirens shattered the silence in the little house.

Just as quickly as the horrible vision had struck, it passed, leaving Elly trembling, her body moist with sweat, her heart pounding erratically in her chest. She covered her eyes with her palms and drew in deep, calming breaths. "It's over. It's over," she whispered until the fear slowly subsided and the pressure in her chest lessened and her brain cleared so that she could think again. Where had she been? What had she been thinking when...

Yes, she reminded herself, *Dan Eastwood.*

She opened her eyes and focused on the long line of gray-green surf on the other side of the sand from where she was parked. She could do this. *She could do this!*

Eastwood. Even if he hadn't refused to answer any more questions, it would be torture to go back and attempt to grill him further. As long as those dark eyes rested on her, Elly knew her mind would wander to that scene on the beach and she'd be incapable of focusing on her job, and—Lord, help her—she might even fall apart as she had just now, only right in front of him. And she couldn't bear that.

The real problem was, although she'd verified several basic points of their investigation she still didn't have enough information to prove he was the one they were looking for.

She looked at her watch. Within a few hours, she'd have to call her father in Elbia with an update. They both knew that if she failed to find the person they were looking for within twenty-four hours, all hell was going to break loose in the international press. The London tabloid that somehow had been leaked information from the palace would reveal a scandal that might threaten the Elbian crown. And Anderson Genealogical Research would earn a very big, very black mark for breaching their own right-to-privacy rule, even if it hadn't been their fault.

Now what was she going to do?

Worrying her bottom lip between her teeth, Elly slid her notebook computer off the passenger seat and into her lap. She flipped open the screen, booted up and summoned the correct file. From memory, she added the information Eastwood had just given her. She had found his name and address through an Internet search, but his mother's phone number and address hadn't come up, probably because she didn't have an e-mail address and her phone number was unlisted.

However, Eastwood had let slip that his mother lived somewhere in the area. "We've been here ever since..." *We,* not I. And he'd offered to take Elly to her, so the woman couldn't be far away.

Elly finished typing her notes then grabbed her purse and locked the car behind her. Neighbors were always a great help in instances such as this, she thought with renewed hope. That was where she'd start.

Elly stood on the top step of the tidy yellow bungalow, straightened her suit jacket, put on a friendly smile, and knocked. It was only a moment before the door opened.

"Yes?" A short, middle-aged woman with blond hair stepped into the opening and gave her a curious smile.

"Margaret Eastwood?" Elly asked.

"Yes, hon." Her accent was pure Bal'morese.

"I was just speaking with your son and—"

The woman's face lit up. "You're a friend of Dan's?"

"Well, not exactly a friend. You see, I was looking for you, but I found Dan's name first and—"

"Come in and tell me why he sent you over." Margaret beamed at her. "This is one of the nicest things about the Haven. A gated community, they call it. You can feel safe chatting with folks, not like in the old neighborhood where we had to be so very careful who we let into the house."

"Well, yes, of course," Elly agreed, feeling just a little guilty, for she was about to become a most unwelcome intruder in this woman's life.

As Elly stepped into the cozy colonial-furnished living room, she focused on a collection of antique glass bottles arranged on shelves in a bay window, then on a display of photographs on top of an upright piano. There were several of a little boy at different ages, babyhood through toddler, then at various school ages. Elly sniffed the air, distracted by a delicious aroma. "Something smells wonderful."

"Gingerbread," Margaret said. "I always make old-fashioned New England gingerbread in the fall. It reminds me of home, and Danny loves it."

"Then you're not from around here?"

"Oh my goodness, no. But Maryland is my home now. I've been here all of my adult life. Sit down, I'll bring you a cup of coffee and a warm slice."

Elly turned around to protest but Margaret was gone.

"You said you've lived here all of your adult life?" she shouted toward the kitchen door.

"In Maryland, not Ocean City. We lived in Baltimore while Dan was young. But he turned into such a beach bum after a few summers of lifeguarding down here. After he was discharged from the service, he wanted me to move down here with him while he attended the community college. Later, he and his friend bought this land and built these cute little cottages." She was beaming proudly as she walked back into the room, holding a tray laden with coffee mugs and plates of fresh gingerbread topped with mountains of whipped cream. "Danny also runs a summer camp for city boys and girls."

"I didn't know that," Elly admitted.

"Oh yes. He feels very strongly about giving inner-city children a few weeks off the streets, to let them see a different world from their troubled neighborhoods."

Elly accepted a steaming mug of coffee and a dessert plate with a second twinge of guilt. She didn't want to deceive this woman who was being so hospitable to her. "Mrs. Eastwood, I have to confess that Dan didn't actually send me over to talk with you."

"Oh?" She looked disappointed.

"I've been hired by a European family to fill in a

missing branch on their family tree. The von Austerands. Do you recognize the name?''

Elly watched as the woman's face grayed and her
fingers pinched nervously at the napkin in her lap.
''No.''

''They're like the Windsors of England. They are
the royal family of a small country that borders on
Austria. Elbia.''

''I think you'd better leave,'' Madge said tightly.

But Elly was determined. She continued choosing
her words carefully. ''We have reason to believe that
a young American woman had a brief romantic liaison
with the young king of that country thirty-three years
ago, before he married. There is a chance that she was
carrying his child when they parted, but if so, she disappeared before the baby was born. Would you know
anything about this, Mrs. Eastwood?''

Dan's mother firmly set her plate on the coffee table
and turned her face toward the rainbow of glass in the
window. ''My husband was an American. His name
was Carl Eastwood, and he died before Dan was a year
old,'' she pronounced tightly.

Carl Eastwood. There it was again, the name Dan
had used. Carl with a C according to the documents
she'd already dug up. Could it be a coincidence that
the young king's name had been Karl? His Royal Highness Karl von Austerand had died just a few years ago,
and now his son Jacob wore his crown. Jacob had always been thought to be the king's sole heir, until evidence of a secret love affair turned up in a routine
cataloguing of the family's papers only days ago. Days
which now felt to Elly like weeks and months of frantic
searching.

"I wouldn't know about affairs or kings or illegitimate royal babies," Madge said sharply.

Elly's heart beat faster despite the woman's denial. Something in her pale eyes told Elly this was a woman unaccustomed to lying, who was desperately trying to do just that.

"I understand how difficult this must be for you," Elly said softly, setting aside her own coffee and fragrant gingerbread to reach across the space between the two chairs and pat the other woman's arm. "But if you can just give me a little more information, please."

Madge's chest rose and fell with labored breaths. She stiffened and leaned back into her chair, her hands gripping the arms. Her features contorted into sharp folds, as if she was trying to work out a difficult puzzle. "Go," she whispered hoarsely. "Get out of my house."

Elly sighed inwardly. She respected the woman's right to privacy, but if she didn't get to the truth soon, both Madge and her son would find themselves in a terrible fix. This was no time for cat-and-mouse games. A simple statement from the woman would save days they didn't have for a full public records' investigation. She'd already picked up and lost two reporters on her way from Connecticut to Baltimore. They might show up at any moment—then it would be out of her hands, if her theory about Dan Eastwood was right. She decided to try a different angle.

"Mrs. Eastwood, I'm not trying to upset you. But in cases where relationships have broken up, the children often *want* to know about their lost family members. Don't you think Dan would like to learn who his real father is?" She was bluffing, just a little, for she wasn't one-hundred-percent certain of all the facts. But if it worked she would know for sure.

Madge's mouth flew wide on a horrified gasp. "My son doesn't need to know—"

Her words stilled in the air as the front door clicked shut and footsteps approached the sitting room from the hall. Both women turned to face the doorway.

Dan Eastwood looked around the corner, his dark eyes glittering dangerously. Even at a distance, Elly could see the thin blue vein throbbing at his temple and the tense cut of his mouth. "I don't need to know *what,* Mother?"

Elly's heart felt as if it were being squeezed by a cold, hard hand. She crossed her fingertips over her chest and swallowed. The warning rumble of Dan's voice sent icy prickles down her spine.

She glanced quickly at Madge, whose expression had altered with amazing speed from a stubborn glare to a helpless pucker. "Oh, dear. I guess I shouldn't have let this young woman in. She told me she was your *girlfriend,* Danny."

Elly gasped in outrage and shot to her feet. The woman wasn't as guileless as she appeared. "I never said that! Mrs. Eastwood, you know that I never implied my visit was—" She let out a frustrated wail. Between his mother and a stranger, who was the man likely to believe? "Never mind. I came alone because I felt your mom might feel less self-conscious speaking to me without your being here."

Dan quirked one skeptical, dark brow at her.

"Honest. I didn't mean any harm."

"I told you I would *bring you* around if necessary!" Dan snapped, then turned to his distraught-looking mother. "I don't know how she found you. I'm sorry. Now, ladies, what is it I *don't* need to know?"

Madge firmly pressed her lips together.

"Then *you* tell me," he stated, swiveling back to Elly.

"At the moment, there may or may not be anything to tell." She was doing her best to be discreet. But Dan was making things harder by the minute, and Madge seemed incapable of saying anything to either stop the truth from coming out or to set facts straight. Elly stood to face him. "It's important that I find out if your mother was ever in Europe…specifically, in Paris."

Dan looked from the woman he'd fantasized about less than an hour earlier, to his mother. He read a level of anxiety in Madge's eyes he had never seen before. "What's going on here, Mom?"

"She's upsetting me," Madge whimpered. "Make her leave."

Dan ground out words between clenched teeth, fighting to hang on to his temper. "She's going to leave as soon as she explains what the hell she's fishing for!"

As infuriating as Elly was, his body still reacted with disturbing warmth to her presence. It was impossible to keep his eyes off her pretty, animated face…or her hands, which kept moving from twin perches on her hips to tug nervously at her blouse's neckline or tuck themselves away when she folded her arms over her chest. Which was another issue entirely…her enticingly lovely, perfectly proportioned chest. She'd evidently left off her jacket for this visit, which offered a much nicer view. Someone help him!

"Why does it matter whether or not my mother ever was in Europe?" he had the presence of mind to demand.

Elly took a deep breath and stepped toward him, praying the right words would come to her. "Papers have recently come to light that indicate a young American woman named Margaret Jennings spent a year abroad, as a student in Paris. That was your maiden name. Right, Mrs. Eastwood?"

Dan answered for her. "Yes, and her junior year she attended the Sorbonne. You told me you did, Mom."

Madge closed her eyes but acknowledged nothing.

Elly held her breath and asked, "Was it during that year that you met a young man named—"

"I met Carl Eastwood there, yes!" Madge snapped, pushing herself up from her armchair with startling energy. "We married, and nine months later Dan was born. But Carl died very young." Tears filled her eyes and she wiped at them with the sleeve of her dress.

Dan frowned, looking more puzzled than ever. "I thought you and Dad hooked up in Baltimore."

"No. No, it was in a little village outside of Paris." Madge sniffled and looked away from her son. "Years later, I heard the church burned down. Probably destroyed all its records too."

Elly opened her mouth to tell the woman she knew that was a lie, but at the last second thought better of it since her six-foot-plus son stood by ready to defend his mother's honor.

"Go on," Dan growled, his too-perceptive gaze locked onto Elly's face. "What were you about to say?"

She swallowed over a sandpaper-dry spot in her throat. "There is no record of a marriage, that's true." She hesitated, but the look on Dan's face told her she must finish what she'd begun, regardless of how he took the news. "There is no record...because there has never been a Carl Eastwood in your mother's life. And there never was a marriage.''

''All right, you're out of here!'' Dan's wide hand shot out. He seized Elly by the arm and marched her firmly toward the door.

She had only enough time to swipe her purse from the coffee table and grab her coat from the back of her chair before he ushered her out of the room.

''I don't know what kind of game you're playing, and I don't care. You're leaving, lady.''

''But don't you want to—''

Before she could get out the rest of her sentence, she found herself standing alone in the cold ocean mist on Madge's lemon-bright porch. She could still feel the pressure of Dan's strong fingers on her arm and his palm on her backside after the door slammed behind her. The nerve of the man. He'd thrown her out!

Then the implication of what had just happened hit her. A triumphant grin spread slowly across her lips.

She had found her missing prince!

Two

Elly bounced in anticipation on the edge of the hotel bed, her ear pressed to the telephone receiver. Someone had gone to find her father to take her call. She'd never seen the castle in person, but photographs of Der Kristallenpalast, the famous crystal palace, revealed an immense, turreted structure of pale, lustrous marble and hundreds of richly appointed rooms. Frank Anderson could easily be half a mile from the nearest phone.

His unmistakable smoker's voice suddenly rasped across the line. "It's about time. What do you have?"

"It's a boy!" she cried.

"The old king had a *son* with the Jennings girl?"

Elly grinned, enjoying her moment of triumph. "That *girl* is now in her fifties, goes by Madge and is being really stubborn about admitting that she had a royal fling thirty-some years ago."

"Understandable," he grumbled. "She married

now? Not wanting her husband to know about her past?''

"No," Elly admitted with a sigh. "But she's sticking to a story about an American husband who died young. I'm certain she made him up for her son's benefit.''

"But you're sure about this young man?"

She hesitated barely a heartbeat. "Yes. Dad, he even looks like Jacob. And the photos of Karl when he was young could be Daniel Eastwood today. They have the same dark hair and strong, angular features, although Eastwood's eyes are dark brown, not blue.''

"That could easily come from the mother's side. Good. I'll tell Jacob.''

"Do we have enough to prove legally he's the old king's son, though?" she asked. She trusted her intuition and the facts she'd uncovered, but the law was another thing.

"Karl was studying at the Sorbonne the same time as Margaret Jennings, according to the school's records. He kept her love letters to him and her farewell note. A handwriting expert can make quick work of comparing this woman's handwriting with that of the person who wrote those letters. There are other documents as well.''

Elly was so excited she could barely speak. But she was also deeply moved by the drama revealed by the decades-old letters they'd found. Those must have been desperate times for a young prince, soon to become king, and his frightened mistress. Had Karl even known that the girl he'd fallen in love with but could never marry carried his child? Nothing they'd found to this date mentioned her pregnancy. How very sad, Elly thought, if the man had died never knowing he had another son.

But now, years later, wonderful things might come of this discovery for Dan and his mother. Not that they deserved it, Elly thought ruefully, tossing her out the way they'd done. But imagine discovering a brother you never knew existed! And a royal one at that!

"What now?" Elly asked her father breathlessly.

"Jacob's advisors told me this morning that if you found the woman and she had a child by the king, they'd want both of them brought over on the first possible plane."

She frowned. "Why?"

"Damage control. They believe that with the pair here in Elbia, the press will have a harder time getting to them. There are also some touchy legal issues to be ironed out, the sooner the better from the crown's perspective."

Elly's mind whirled, and she felt short of breath. "Eastwood doesn't even believe me. How will I get him on a plane to Europe? Dad, this isn't our job. All we agreed to do was verify historical records. We're not private investigators."

"Elizabeth." His chastising papa-bear growl ended in a soft cough. She hated that he smoked. But since her mother had died there had been no one, including herself, who could talk sense to the man about his health or anything else.

"Well, we're not!" she insisted.

"We have no choice at this point. The king blames us for the leak. He's absolutely convinced that no one in his court would peddle such volatile news to the press. Now we have to do what we can to save a bad situation. And—" He balked.

"There's more bad news?" She didn't want to think about one more complication.

"Consider the many implications of this discovery, Elly. There is enormous wealth at stake. Even an illegitimate child might demand a portion of his father's fortune. And what about the mother? As far as we know, she has never been compensated for her pregnancy or given any financial help in raising the boy."

Elly rolled her eyes to the motel room's chalky ceiling. The packet of letters her father had only recently discovered hidden behind a panel in an ancient armoire had turned into a modern Pandora's box. In addition to the love notes, signed "adoringly, Margaret," other letters, returned from the United States as undeliverable, indicated that over the next ten years Karl had tried to locate his lost love, but failed. Perhaps it was just his beloved Margaret he searched for. Or maybe he feared the existence of a child and knew the danger an illegitimate offspring, older by several months than his son by the queen, would pose to his dynasty.

"Get them on a plane," Elly repeated dully, shaking her head. "Short of kidnapping mother and son, I'm not sure how I'll manage that."

"We don't have much time," Frank reminded her. "If I were that young man or his mother, I'd want to find a good place to hide out for a while. The press will eat them alive."

Elly shook her head. "Something tells me this guy isn't the type to run away from anything."

"Elizabeth," her father whispered hoarsely, sounding increasingly worried, "if this explodes in our faces, our professional reputation will be destroyed. We might as well give up the business. *Do you understand?*"

She swallowed. It was that bad then. "I'll bring them to you," she promised. "Somehow."

Dan was thirty minutes late for his appointment with the contractor, mostly because he had other things on his mind. His thoughts boomeranged back and forth between memories of manhandling an attractive redhead out his mother's door, his hand placed strategically on her pretty rump, and the less enjoyable knowledge that he'd probably never see Elly Anderson again.

Luckily, the contractor was still in his office. They negotiated a few terms, signed the contract. Within a week the storm damage to the bungalows closest to the shoreline would be repaired. One less thing to worry about.

Dan drove back toward the Haven along Ocean Avenue and turned into the parking lot. A flash of crimson hair in the sunlight caught his eye. Setting the parking brake on his SUV, he squinted through the windshield into the wintry glare. A man and a woman stood where the lot met the sandy boardwalk.

Elly's elegant legs appeared even longer whenever the wind flipped up the hem of her skirt. Her hair, lifting free of confining pins, swirled in russet waves around her face as she talked to Kevin and occasionally lifted a hand to hold flaming wisps out of her eyes.

"What's that woman up to now?" he muttered, heaving himself up out of the car.

Dear old Kev wore that deer-staring-into-headlights expression common to men confronted by a pretty woman. Dan only hoped his friend hadn't said anything to encourage Elly's snooping. He jogged across the parking lot toward them.

"I thought we agreed you were through with this nonsense!" Dan shouted into the wind.

Elly turned to observe him, her eyes far too enticing to cool his simmering blood. Simmering because he was furious with her but also because she looked so deliciously disheveled with the wind tugging at her skirt and hair, and teasing open the collar of her jacket to reveal a sliver of flesh at the top of her breast.

She planted her feet firmly and straightened her spine to meet him. "We need to talk, Mr. Eastwood."

"Isn't that where we started this morning?"

Kevin looked from one to the other of them with a puzzled expression then backed off two steps. "I don't know what this is about, but I'll let you two hash things out. Got work to do."

To Dan's surprise, Elly didn't so much as blink or make any move that might be construed as retreat. "I need you and Mrs. Eastwood on a plane for Europe," she stated. "Tonight at the latest."

He laughed. "You're not only wrong about my mother, you're insane!"

"No," she said solemnly, "I'm not. Not on either account. I have evidence. Please listen to me. If you don't, both of you are going to be hurt far more than you can imagine."

There was something fervent and beyond argument in her tone. This was a woman who believed in what she said. For the first time Dan felt deep in his gut that Elizabeth Anderson wasn't flinging idle fairy tales at him or working some kind of confidence game. He remembered the look on his mother's face earlier that day. Madge had been afraid—not of lies, but of the *truth*. And that terrified him.

He looked at his watch. "It's getting close to lunch time. Are you hungry?"

Elly gave him a guarded look. "Famished," she admitted. "No time for breakfast this morning. Why?"

"Let's get a table at Kirby's. We can talk this out over crab cakes."

Kirby's, one of the most popular seafood restaurants on Ocean Avenue, was nearly deserted during off season. They sat in a fifties-style red vinyl booth and Dan ordered two steaming crab cake platters piled high with salty French fries, little paper cups of sweet coleslaw on the side.

Elly poured a stream of rich ketchup over her fries and dug in hungrily. Dan ate more slowly than usual, watching her. He was aware of her thin ankles crossed beneath the table, visible through the space between his bench and the table top. When he lifted his eyes they fixed with fascination on her animated lips as she relished the crunchy potatoes and fat crab cake with its savory Old Bay seasonings perfuming the room around them.

He found it impossible to hold onto his irritation with her. But he *was* curious and more than a little suspicious of her motives for wanting to whisk him off to another continent. "So tell me about this proof. And why the urgency to get me out of the country?"

"I know you feel I'm intruding," she began, spearing another fry with her fork and shaking it at him in schoolmarm fashion, "and I don't like being put in the position of having to accuse anyone of lying about their past but—"

"But that's precisely what you are doing, isn't it?" he asked in a low voice.

Elly pursed her lips and studied him for a long moment, as if searching for diplomatic words. "People can be very creative about their past, if they are afraid. A woman has to be particularly careful. And a single mom *always* has to explain herself to others. No doubt your mother felt that a dead husband was easier for people to accept than the truth."

"And that truth is?" He might be willing to believe her. *Might.* But not without one hell of an explanation.

Elly continued with obvious caution as she pulled a manila envelope from the briefcase on the bench beside her. "I have photocopies of letters found on the von Austerand family's property. There now is little doubt that the ones signed *Margaret* were written by your mother, but we can verify that as soon as she is in Elbia."

She put up a hand to stop him from interrupting. "We believe your mother fell deeply in love with Karl von Austerand the year she studied in Paris. She probably believed they would marry, but he wasn't completely honest with her. He was engaged to another woman of royal blood. And he was the crown prince, soon to become King of Elbia.

"Karl was attending the college under an assumed name to avoid publicity. When Madge discovered they could never wed, she ran home to America—probably just after learning she was pregnant. Instead of returning to her parents' home in Massachusetts, she found a place to live in Baltimore and hid her shame by inventing a husband. The move probably was intended to elude Karl, too. Perhaps she feared what he might do if he discovered their child. *You.*"

Dan could feel the heat rising from his chest to his throat. He glared at the folder resting on the table be-

so hard to hide from him, from her
hbors, from the world. This would kill

mbly at Elly across the table. "We
his."
t I promise you, my father and I had
with letting your mother's past become
dge. And now we'll do everything we
th you and Madge weather the storm."
you intend to do? Wave a magic wand
disappear?"
im another one of those delicious enig-
"Something like that."

elieved when Dan told her he would agree
er to Elbia. But convincing his mother to
comfy cottage was, at first, a struggle.
he first phone call from a *Washington Star*

ly the British press who had first been
nformation had contacted several American
s in their search for the missing prince of
Star put a team on the story and soon it was
he prying phone calls were destined to be-
more harassing visits. Madge was so hor-
he prospect of her home being invaded she
y agreed to the trip.
elp from the Elbian embassy, Elly booked all
hem on the Concorde for that night. On their
the Eastern Shore of Maryland to Dulles Air-
/ashington, D.C., they somehow picked up two
of reporters. "It's all right," Elly assured a
d Madge, "as long as we keep moving, they

neath her hand. "This is very difficult to believe," he
said tightly.

Elly slowly shook her head. "I'm sorry. See for
yourself."

He couldn't move, was barely capable of breathing.
Still furious with Elly, he was nevertheless increasingly
fearful that what she claimed might be true. She didn't
have to tell him how drastically his life would change
if it was.

And what about Madge's quiet existence? She hated
confrontation. She had always favored a life without
complications. Any shattered love affair and unwanted
baby were as complicated as life got. Unless the father
of your baby was a man whose family's status rivaled
that of the royals of England or Monaco—people with
unlimited wealth and power, who could never escape
their celebrity or stay off the front page of grocery-
store gossip rags for long.

Elly rested her warm hand over his on the tabletop.
"This must be a shock to you. You've grown up believing one thing, and here I am telling you everything
is different. I'm sorry. Truly, I am." Her eyes shone
with sincerity and compassion. "I would have preferred to let your mother keep her secret. But it's out
of my hands now. Others have found out, so you both
needed to know."

He couldn't utter a word. His lips felt as stiff as if
he'd climbed from a December ocean.

"Take your time reading while you finish eating,"
she offered. "Then let me know what you think." Her
accent was flavored with New England. Maple-syrup
sweet, with a touch of Yankee logic. He would have
liked to get to know her better, a whole lot better. She
seemed a nice person, in addition to being so easy on

the eyes. But it appeared that more pressing matters were on deck.

Dan took a bite of his cooling crab cake and chewed without tasting anything, then studied her as she sipped her cola. "There's a lot riding on this, isn't there? I mean, aside from being hounded by the press."

She slanted him a look that would have done the Mona Lisa proud. "There might be."

Dan slipped a thin stack of photocopies from the envelope. He scanned the first report quickly:

Daniel Robert Jennings. Born August 20, 1970. Verified location of birth: Baltimore, Maryland. Birth certificate on record. Mother: Margaret Jennings. No father listed. Name of mother and child legally changed three months later: Eastwood. Reason given: marriage to Carl Eastwood. No Carl Eastwood match through public records. Internet search unsuccessful. Social Security source reports no matches for location and dates given. Results: Suspect fictitious name.

There were other reports, which he read hastily, his pulse throbbing in his temple, his mouth going stone dry…

Margaret Jennings, scholarship student at the Sorbonne, 1969-1970. Superior student. Dropped out of school 3/70. Reason given: personal.

Frigid droplets of sweat skittered down the back of his neck. He stared at the next page's remarks: "Love letters signed 'your adoring Margaret,' no envelopes." There were even photocopies of two of the letters. He

tried not to th
the words, wl
by other than
only to glance
ingly similar to
another notation

Letters from H
and to one Mar
dated 1970 (3),
1980—all retur

"Well?" Elly as
empty plate.

He smiled weakly
might be a little n
yours."

"More than nervo
born before he was."

"Ouch."

"It gets worse," she
palace leaked rumors of
photographer are hot on
ing me, but I shook ther
luck that I found you bef

Dan no longer felt hungr
Visions of TV cameras, re
phones and endless telepho
hawks flooded his imaginati
to tell himself that it might b
licity for the Haven and his

A second later, reality smad
It wouldn't be his property or
would get all the attention. It

38

past she'd tried
friends and neig
her.

He stared n
didn't ask for t

"I know. B
nothing to do
public knowle
can to help b

"What do
and make us

She gave h
matic smiles.

Elly was r
to go with h
evacuate he
Then came
reporter.

Apparent
leaked the
newspaper
Elbia. The
clear that
come eve
rified at t
reluctantl

With h
three of t
way fron
port in V
carloads
frighten

can't get to you. And State Department security is waiting for us at the airport."

The limousine she had ordered raced the two black sedans through twisting roadways approaching the international terminals, then the three of them were led to a lounge where security guards kept the press at bay while they waited to board the plane. Soon, a State Department courier arrived with passports for Dan and his mother, and minutes later they were herded onto the immense jet without being accosted. She felt like giving a victory cheer. But as the sleek, tipped-nose Concorde took off with a gentle rumble into the night, Elly sensed they'd only temporarily eluded their troubles.

The seating on the Concorde felt far more spacious than that on most commercial flights. Elly had never flown on the famous French-built jet that only the elite of the world could afford. Two roomy seats were positioned on either side of the aisle, and the service was impeccably attentive. Madge and Dan sat on one side. Elly was on the opposite side of the aisle, at the window seat, while the place beside her remained empty.

After they'd taken off into the night, Elly closed her eyes for a moment. Exhaustion overcame her. She felt weightless; her mind drifted. Back to another time in her life. A time when there had been more than just two Andersons. Elly, Dad…Mom. She felt herself being sucked back in time as she pictured her mother's face smiling down at her. Elly fought the memories, struggled to escape from the images that kept her from finding peace in her own life. Her heart began to race. Her breaths came in short, shallow puffs as the muscles in her chest constricted. Resisting was futile…

"It's going to be all right, Elly," her mother had

promised when Elly became concerned that her baby brother might come at night while Elly slept. Then she'd miss all the excitement. "It's all planned. The doctor will meet me at the hospital on the date you and I wrote on the calendar. Remember? I'll have an operation called a cesarean section to take the baby from my tummy. You'll be able to see him minutes after he's born, then you and I will fight over who gets to cuddle him."

They'd laughed together over that. Her father had told Elly that, at twelve years of age, she was almost old enough to be a little mother herself, at least in some cultures in other parts of the world. Even before the baby's seventh month of gestation, she had begun to feel her little brother in her arms, to sense a growing protectiveness of him and know that they would be a wonderful family together—the four of them.

Then the half sleep she'd sunk into on the plane dragged her deeper into darker memories. Of *that* night.

Again she was tortured by Patricia Anderson's agonized screams and her father's shouts for help to the 911 operator. When she'd tried to go to her mother, Frank had blocked her from the bedroom, shouting frantically at her that she couldn't go in, shoving her back into her own room as if she were being punished for a crime she didn't understand.

Blue and red lights flashed in the street outside her window. She'd watched two paramedics rush into the house while the driver pulled a gurney from the ambulance. "She will be okay," she whispered to herself. "Daddy said so." But minutes passed and the ambulance still sat there. Soon Elly knew, without being neath her hand. "This is very difficult to believe," he said tightly.

Elly slowly shook her head. "I'm sorry. See for yourself."

He couldn't move, was barely capable of breathing. Still furious with Elly, he was nevertheless increasingly fearful that what she claimed might be true. She didn't have to tell him how drastically his life would change if it was.

And what about Madge's quiet existence? She hated confrontation. She had always favored a life without complications. Any shattered love affair and unwanted baby were as complicated as life got. Unless the father of your baby was a man whose family's status rivaled that of the royals of England or Monaco—people with unlimited wealth and power, who could never escape their celebrity or stay off the front page of grocery-store gossip rags for long.

Elly rested her warm hand over his on the tabletop. "This must be a shock to you. You've grown up believing one thing, and here I am telling you everything is different. I'm sorry. Truly, I am." Her eyes shone with sincerity and compassion. "I would have preferred to let your mother keep her secret. But it's out of my hands now. Others have found out, so you both needed to know."

He couldn't utter a word. His lips felt as stiff as if he'd climbed from a December ocean.

"Take your time reading while you finish eating," she offered. "Then let me know what you think." Her accent was flavored with New England. Maple-syrup sweet, with a touch of Yankee logic. He would have liked to get to know her better, a whole lot better. She seemed a nice person, in addition to being so easy on

the eyes. But it appeared that more pressing matters
were on deck.

Dan took a bite of his cooling crab cake and chewed
without tasting anything, then studied her as she sipped
her cola. ''There's a lot riding on this, isn't there? I
mean, aside from being hounded by the press.''

She slanted him a look that would have done the
Mona Lisa proud. ''There might be.''

Dan slipped a thin stack of photocopies from the
envelope. He scanned the first report quickly:

> Daniel Robert Jennings. Born August 20, 1970.
> Verified location of birth: Baltimore, Maryland.
> Birth certificate on record. Mother: Margaret Jen-
> nings. No father listed. Name of mother and child
> legally changed three months later: Eastwood.
> Reason given: marriage to Carl Eastwood. No
> Carl Eastwood match through public records. In-
> ternet search unsuccessful. Social Security source
> reports no matches for location and dates given.
> Results: Suspect fictitious name.

There were other reports, which he read hastily, his
pulse throbbing in his temple, his mouth going stone
dry...

> Margaret Jennings, scholarship student at the Sor-
> bonne, 1969–1970. Superior student. Dropped out
> of school 3/70. Reason given: personal.

Frigid droplets of sweat skittered down the back of
his neck. He stared at the next page's remarks: ''Love
letters signed 'your adoring Margaret,' no envelopes.''
There were even photocopies of two of the letters. He

tried not to think about the passion and longing behind the words, which seemed far too personal to be read by other than the two people involved. But he needed only to glance at the handwriting to know it was amazingly similar to Madge's flowery style. Then there was another notation:

Letters from His Royal Highness Karl von Auster-
and to one Margaret Jennings in the United States,
dated 1970 (3), 1972 (2), 1973, 1975, 1976 and
1980—all returned as undeliverable.

"Well?" Elly asked, glancing up at him from her empty plate.

He smiled weakly. "I imagine Karl's legitimate son might be a little nervous about this discovery of yours."

"More than nervous. Particularly since you were born before he was."

"Ouch."

"It gets worse," she assured him. "Somebody in the palace leaked rumors of the affair. A reporter and his photographer are hot on your trail. They were following me, but I shook them off in Baltimore. It's only luck that I found you before they did."

Dan no longer felt hungry. He pushed his plate away. Visions of TV cameras, reporters armed with microphones and endless telephone calls from pushy media hawks flooded his imagination. For an instant he tried to tell himself that it might be a good thing—free publicity for the Haven and his City Kids program.

A second later, reality smacked him upside his head. It wouldn't be his property or his favorite charity that would get all the attention. It would be Madge and the past she'd tried so hard to hide from him, from her friends and neighbors, from the world. This would kill her.

He stared numbly at Elly across the table. "We didn't ask for this."

"I know. But I promise you, my father and I had nothing to do with letting your mother's past become public knowledge. And now we'll do everything we can to help both you and Madge weather the storm."

"What do you intend to do? Wave a magic wand and make us disappear?"

She gave him another one of those delicious enigmatic smiles. "Something like that."

Elly was relieved when Dan told her he would agree to go with her to Elbia. But convincing his mother to evacuate her comfy cottage was, at first, a struggle. Then came the first phone call from a *Washington Star* reporter.

Apparently the British press who had first been leaked the information had contacted several American newspapers in their search for the missing prince of Elbia. The *Star* put a team on the story and soon it was clear that the prying phone calls were destined to become even more harassing visits. Madge was so horrified at the prospect of her home being invaded she reluctantly agreed to the trip.

With help from the Elbian embassy, Elly booked all three of them on the Concorde for that night. On their way from the Eastern Shore of Maryland to Dulles Airport in Washington, D.C., they somehow picked up two carloads of reporters. "It's all right," Elly assured a frightened Madge, "as long as we keep moving, they can't get to you. And State Department security is waiting for us at the airport.''

The limousine she had ordered raced the two black sedans through twisting roadways approaching the international terminals, then the three of them were led to a lounge where security guards kept the press at bay while they waited to board the plane. Soon, a State Department courier arrived with passports for Dan and his mother, and minutes later they were herded onto the immense jet without being accosted. She felt like giving a victory cheer. But as the sleek, tipped-nose Concorde took off with a gentle rumble into the night, Elly sensed they'd only temporarily eluded their troubles.

The seating on the Concorde felt far more spacious than that on most commercial flights. Elly had never flown on the famous French-built jet that only the elite of the world could afford. Two roomy seats were positioned on either side of the aisle, and the service was impeccably attentive. Madge and Dan sat on one side. Elly was on the opposite side of the aisle, at the window seat, while the place beside her remained empty.

After they'd taken off into the night, Elly closed her eyes for a moment. Exhaustion overcame her. She felt weightless; her mind drifted. Back to another time in her life. A time when there had been more than just two Andersons. Elly, Dad…Mom. She felt herself being sucked back in time as she pictured her mother's face smiling down at her. Elly fought the memories, struggled to escape from the images that kept her from finding peace in her own life. Her heart began to race. Her breaths came in short, shallow puffs as the muscles in her chest constricted. Resisting was futile…

''It's going to be all right, Elly,'' her mother had

promised when Elly became concerned that her baby brother might come at night while Elly slept. Then she'd miss all the excitement. "It's all planned. The doctor will meet me at the hospital on the date you and I wrote on the calendar. Remember? I'll have an operation called a cesarean section to take the baby from my tummy. You'll be able to see him minutes after he's born, then you and I will fight over who gets to cuddle him."

They'd laughed together over that. Her father had told Elly that, at twelve years of age, she was almost old enough to be a little mother herself, at least in some cultures in other parts of the world. Even before the baby's seventh month of gestation, she had begun to feel her little brother in her arms, to sense a growing protectiveness of him and know that they would be a wonderful family together—the four of them.

Then the half sleep she'd sunk into on the plane dragged her deeper into darker memories. Of *that* night.

Again she was tortured by Patricia Anderson's agonized screams and her father's shouts for help to the 911 operator. When she'd tried to go to her mother, Frank had blocked her from the bedroom, shouting frantically at her that she couldn't go in, shoving her back into her own room as if she were being punished for a crime she didn't understand.

Blue and red lights flashed in the street outside her window. She'd watched two paramedics rush into the house while the driver pulled a gurney from the ambulance. "She will be okay," she whispered to herself. "Daddy said so." But minutes passed and the ambulance still sat there. Soon Elly knew, without being told, that when they did bring her mother out it wouldn't be to take her to the hospital.

Elly heard a whimper and something moist trickled down her cheeks. She twisted violently in her seat, felt the heaviness in her chest pressing relentlessly, then sensed a warm hand settling on her shoulder.

"Are you all right?" It wasn't her mother's voice, as she'd so often imagined at the end of her worst attacks. This voice had a deeper, stronger timbre. "Elly?"

She blinked her eyes open and took a moment to orient herself to an adult world, lights dim along a slender, shining cabin. Her throat burned, and her temples throbbed hotly. Turning her head, she looked up at Dan who had crossed the aisle to sit in the vacant seat beside her.

"You were having a bad dream," he murmured.

"Was I?" The break between the past and the present seemed liquid, as if she still might float back into the pain and experience it all over again.

Dan took her hand between his and rested it on his knee. "Want to tell me about it? If you share a dream, you can keep it from coming back, you know." He smiled at her.

"Not this one." She shivered then swallowed twice, trying to ease the roughness in her throat, trying to calm her drumming heartbeat. Horrid sounds still reverberated in her head. The awful coldness of death clutched at her. "This one's a keeper, whether I want it or not."

Dan frowned. "A bad one, huh?"

"The worst." She would have let it go at that. But his quiet compassion and steady gaze beckoned her to say more. She had a sudden intuitive flash that she and

Dan shared something—pasts that would haunt them and remain with them all of their lives. "It's not fantasy," she explained. "It's like an instant replay of something that really happened."

"Like a soldier having a flashback of battle?"

"Something like that." Elly drew herself up in the seat, still trembling, and glanced across at Madge. She was fast asleep. "You're really good to her," she whispered.

"Why shouldn't I be? She's my mother."

"Some people don't appreciate what they have, the sacrifices their parents make for them."

"I guess that's true," he agreed slowly, encouraging her with his steady gaze. "Aren't you good to your mother?"

Her eyes closed. She shuddered.

"I'm sorry," Dan whispered. "That was far too personal." He took a deep breath. "I suppose I felt justified, since you've dug up so much about me. I know nothing of you, except that you work for your father."

She shrugged, feeling a little calmer at the sound of his mellow voice. "There's not a lot to tell. I was twelve years old. My parents had tried for years to have a second child. They were overjoyed when it looked as if my mother would carry to full term." Her voice was flat, without the emotion she held so carefully within her. "Mom died in childbirth. My baby brother didn't make it either."

"That's terrible." He squeezed her hand. "It must have taken a long time to get over that." Then their eyes met and he knew. "Or maybe you never have."

She looked away from his too-perceptive gaze. The thick-glassed window to her left was black. No moon. But fat, white stars shone through the night over the endless Atlantic Ocean. She felt Dan's thumb drawing comforting circles over the back of her hand.

Suddenly, Elly found herself talking. Pushing out words without taking a breath, baring her soul as she'd never done with anyone in her life. She couldn't imagine why everything should tumble out of her at this moment, in front of this man. Perhaps because she foresaw pain and a struggle coming his way. Or maybe it was because they would soon go their separate ways. Sharing the agony of her past and fears of the future with this man who was passing so briefly through her life was as devoid of threat as confiding in a wall.

As she let the words flow, telling him of the night she had lost her mother forever and her father for many months to his grief, Dan's arm came around her, as if to shield her from her own memories.

"My dad just stopped functioning after my mother died. He didn't go to work. He didn't eat enough to keep a person alive. He started smoking again, and he drank quite a lot, I think. He spent a lot of time away— most of every day and always the nights. He wouldn't mention her name. We didn't talk."

Dan stared at her, his eyes hard and dark with concern. "That was when you most needed him."

She sighed. "Yes, but I can't blame him for distancing himself from me. If you ever saw my mother's college graduation photo, you'd think that I could be her twin. It just hurt Dad too much to look at me, and think about her."

"That's no excuse for neglecting a child," he snapped.

She squeezed her eyes shut. "You can't understand how it was." She swallowed. Dare she go on? Dare she tell him the rest, the part that still controlled her future and wouldn't let her move on with her own life? But now that she'd opened her soul to him it seemed impossible to stop the flood of feelings.

"Years later," she whispered, "Dad told me what had happened that night. My mother had an enlarged heart. They'd known that since I was born and had elected to do a C-section. Her doctor had advised another C-section to take the stress off delivering her second baby. When she went into labor early, her heart couldn't take it, and the baby died of asphyxiation before the medics could arrive." She swallowed three times before she was able to look at him again. Tears clung to her eyelashes.

"I'm so sorry, Elly."

She nodded, plunging on. "Dad insisted that I get a complete physical a few years later. He didn't seem surprised when they found I'd inherited my mother's heart problem, it was just a little larger than it should have been. Nothing easily fixed, just something to live cautiously with.

"From that day, I decided never to have children of my own. I love kids, I really do," she insisted, her heart breaking even as she said the words. "But I can't risk my life the way my mother did."

"Death in childbirth is a very rare thing these days," Dan commented gently. "Chances are, if she'd been able to reach a hospital, she'd have been all right. You shouldn't—"

Elly pulled her hand away from him. "Don't tell me what I should or shouldn't do!" she snapped. Not wanting to alarm the sleeping passengers around them, she choked back the sob that swelled inside her. The words came out in breathless gulps. *"Don't…lecture…me!"*

"I'm not, Elly," he whispered. "I'm just trying to state a medical reality. All sorts of advances have been made in the last ten or more years. Odds are that if you really want a baby, you could have one without complications."

She glared at him. "Odds. Chances. Do you really believe that adding one more child to this earth is worth the risk to me or any other woman whose body isn't strong enough?"

He didn't answer.

She let out a long breath, feeling strangely better for the release of emotions. She thought more clearly now about her past choices.

Over the years, she'd had a few male friends—mostly kept at arm's length with no physical relationship involved. A few she'd slept with, but only after first being sure they lacked all desire to settle down and start a family, then guaranteeing she couldn't become pregnant with them. She had stayed on the Pill during those limited months in a relationship and, because she'd never given her heart, she hadn't regretted when they'd moved on to other women. The last breakup had been heart-wrenching, though. Sam had been a good person and she'd grown intensely fond of him. His only crime was that he'd changed his mind. He had decided he wanted to be a husband and father instead of a boyfriend.

In the year since then Elly had let no one into her life. But sitting beside her now was a man who was as much temptation as any woman could handle. More than *she* could, she feared. Instinctively, she gauged the level of her reaction to him, and knew that the passion centered in the core of her being was new and real and strong. He had touched something in her no other man before him had been capable of, although they'd known each other only hours.

"What about you?" she asked quickly. "Why aren't you married?" A tiny part of her hoped that his answer would be an echo of her own. *I don't want kids.*

"I suppose at first I was too involved with other facets of my life," he admitted. "The marines—that didn't seem a time for settling down. I was stationed all over the place. Then I went to college on the GI Bill and earned my degree. After that I needed time to start my business. I've always wanted a family, but now that it seems the right time, the right woman doesn't seem to be around."

She cringed inside. Well, there it was. He was looking for a life-mate, a mother for his unborn children. *And I am definitely not her,* she thought with an irrational twinge of sadness. Yet Elly was still profoundly attracted to him. He set off tickly sensations in parts of her body she had forgotten existed.

Dan squeezed her softly around the shoulders and she looked up into his concerned gaze. "Feeling better?"

"Yes," she admitted half-heartedly. "I'll be fine. Thank you for lending your shoulder." She patted the damp fabric of his blazer.

He glanced back at his own seat across the aisle. Madge had repositioned herself, lifting her legs to rest them across his cushion. Like many of the other passengers, she was asleep.

"Mind if I stay here for a while?"

Elly nodded. "No problem. She'll need her strength when we get to Elbia."

They talked through most of the night, keeping the conversation light. It was as if they both understood that much of what they'd already shared was too personal for people who had just met. But somehow, Elly thought, it had been the right time to speak of such things.

The jet landed at Orly, outside Paris, soon after dawn. The reporters who had tailed them to Dulles hadn't been able to keep up with them at the Concorde's pace, even if they had managed to find another flight on a traditional plane. But they must have alerted their cohorts, for the paparazzi jostled each other for position at the concourse entrance.

"Oh dear," Madge whimpered, "how will we ever get past them?"

Elly pointed to a cluster of French gendarmes looking over the disembarking passengers. "Looks like the palace has been in touch with authorities here. Let's go." She took Madge's arm and led her forward. Dan followed close behind.

The security team whisked them into a car that veered quickly away to a private runway. A high-speed helicopter marked with the von Austerand royal crest lifted them away and, just two hours later, Elly drew a sharp breath at the sight of the Crystal Palace as they flew over the mountains separating Austria from Elbia. Below, and surrounding the magnificent towers and crenellated parapets, was the storybook city of the same name whose history reached back into medieval times.

Madge uttered a cry of delight at the sight. "How beautiful." Tears filled her eyes. She looked sadly at her son and shouted over the roar of the rotors above them. "Do you hate me, Danny, for keeping this from you all these years?"

He patted her arm and shook his head vehemently. "You gave me a warm, safe childhood," he yelled back, smiling. But as soon as his mother turned back to the view, his expression tightened.

Elly spoke directly into his ear. "What's wrong?"

"Later," he mouthed.

She nodded, guessing his thoughts. Madge hadn't kept a royal upbringing and a title from her son. Tradition and politics had done that. She would never have been allowed to bring her child to this magnificent place. The appearance of Karl's mistress and illegitimate son would have been an insult to the queen. At most, Elly suspected, Karl might have offered to pay for the baby's care and for Madge's silence. Dan's mother must have understood this. She had chosen not to be found by him. She had turned her back on her lover's charity...or bribe, whichever it might be.

Elly grasped these truths with an intuitive sense shared by all females. When fate conspired against a woman, her pride was all that saved her, if she was to survive at all. And now Elly knew she must do whatever she could to protect both Madge and Dan, for, in a way, she was responsible for their troubles. If she and her father hadn't unwittingly revealed information to the wrong person, the press wouldn't even now be on their trail.

Three

It was at dinner that night, in one of the castle's more intimate dining halls, that Elly finally met the royal family. She and her father had walked together from their rooms in a separate wing of the castle. They found Dan and Madge already there with a dozen other guests, standing with cocktails in hand. Elly accepted a glass of white wine from a steward, crossed the room to join them and introduced her father to mother and son.

"Who are all these other people?" Dan asked.

Frank looked around, then back to Dan. "Jacob's court, and his political, financial and cultural advisors. They're here to check you out and decide what to do about you." He gave Dan a wry smile and lifted his glass in an ironic toast. "Not to put any pressure on you, my boy."

Dan scanned the room warily. The muscles in his

neck stood out in taut relief above his shirt collar. "Why don't they come right out and say what they're thinking?"

"They don't know what to think yet," Elly said softly. "You're a wild card. No one knows whether you'll threaten Jacob's rule, demand a fortune for yourself and your mother or just prove to be an embarrassment."

"I already told you I don't want anything!" Dan snapped.

Elly wondered if he was really that irritated with the Elbians or just in a bad mood for any of a number of reasons—like being forced to fly halfway around the world at a few hours' notice. She turned to Madge, who was sipping delicately from a crystal stem. "What about you, Mrs. Eastwood? What do you want out of all this?"

"I want to go home," she said solemnly, then closed her lips tightly and looked away.

Elly imagined the woman did miss the cozy safety of her little bungalow. The palace was intimidating with its hundreds of rooms full of priceless antique furnishings and exquisite art collections. It was like living in the Louvre. "Maybe you'll feel differently once you meet the king and queen," she said encouragingly.

"They are gracious and fair people," Frank put in.

Madge nodded her willingness to give them a chance, but she still looked uneasy.

Dan observed his mother with obvious concern. He looked no more convinced of the royal pair's good will than she did.

Elly wished she could think of a way to steer him toward a more receptive frame of mind for meeting his half brother. But before she could say anything else, the immense gilded doors at the far end of the room swung wide. An attendant in full livery stepped through. He stood as straight and silent as one of the palace guards while conversation hushed and the roomful of guests turned to face him.

"Announcing Their Royal Highnesses, King Jacob von Austerand and Queen Allison..." There followed a long list of formal titles for the royal couple. Elly's heart beat in triple time, and a thrill rushed through her as Elbia's young rulers entered the room.

Jacob was strikingly handsome in a stoic way. He didn't appear to be the type of man to smile very often, but when he did, Elly imagined he'd light up any woman's heart. His hair was a glistening ebony, and his eyes flashed midnight blue.

As to his queen, Elly had never seen a more beautiful woman. The young American who had married Jacob wore her pale-blond hair coiled softly on top of her head, anchored with a crown that would never be mistaken for the rhinestone-studded ornaments worn by hometown beauty queens. White diamonds blazed upon gold in an intricate filigree pattern. Elly vaguely remembered TV news clips about the couple—how the young prince had caused constitutional upheaval in his little country when he had insisted on wedding a commoner, and an American on top of that. But somehow the two of them had weathered the political storm, and they seemed at peace in their marriage now.

Queen Allison smiled sweetly at her guests, lavishing attention on each person in the room as her fingertips rested lightly on the back of her husband's extended hand.

As Jacob and his queen crossed the room, the king's gaze swept impatiently across faces until they settled on Dan's. A sharp questioning look blazed across his eyes but was quickly obscured by an official smile.

He stopped in front of the four of them—Elly, Frank, Dan and Madge. They performed the traditional bows and curtseys as they'd been instructed to do by the palace's protocol officer. Dan's bow, Elly noticed, was no more than a slight forward tilt of his body, and he wasn't smiling. The distrust between the two men was uncomfortably evident.

Elly's heart raced with apprehension as her father made the introductions.

"You had a pleasant journey?" Jacob asked politely.

Dan gave a stiff nod. "Uneventful."

"I've been told you had company on your way to the airport," Allison commented, her voice softly soothing. "I hope the reporters didn't frighten you, Mrs. Eastwood." She looked with compassion toward Madge.

Dan spoke before his mother could answer. "A lot of commotion over nothing, if you ask me."

"Really?" Jacob's perfect English was accented with harsh Germanic tones and clipped consonants. "You think that claiming a monarch as your father is a small thing then?"

Dan shifted his shoulders and met Jacob's hostile stare with equal intensity. "Look, Your Highness, less than forty-eight hours ago, I was taking my morning swim and planning my work day, oblivious to the existence of this postage stamp of a country. I didn't ask for this, and I'm not *claiming* anything. It's other people who are all in a lather about this situation, not me."

Elly held her breath as Jacob studied his half brother through blue-black eyes that sparked with displeasure. All conversation in the room had ceased. She suspected

Jacob had the authority to do whatever he pleased within the confines of his little kingdom, and perhaps beyond it. A man with that much power could be dangerous.

The young king turned abruptly to Madge. "Is it true that you were my father's mistress?" Tact, apparently, was not one of Jacob's strong points.

Madge blushed, and her hand shook, spilling a little of her wine.

"Now hold on!" Dan barked, his face flaring red with anger.

The queen's hand moved almost imperceptibly up her husband's arm in a cautionary gesture. Jacob shot a quick look out of the corner of his eyes at her, and she lifted a brow.

"I'm sorry," Jacob said awkwardly. "I'm being far too direct. It's just that we've all been turned on end by this discovery. My subjects worry about their 'postage stamp of a country,' as you put it." He shot Dan a cold look. "They need to be reassured that their government isn't in danger of—"

Dan laughed out loud. "What the hell do they think I'm going to do? Storm the castle?"

Jacob did not smile. "You can't possibly comprehend the seriousness of this situation."

Dan bristled. "And I don't think you understand what your interference might do to *my* business! Not to mention to my mother's privacy."

Elly shot a quick look at Madge, whose lips were compressed in a pale line. Allison's hand moved away from her husband's arm and she looked apologetically into Elly's eyes, as if to say, *I'm sorry. This is something I cannot interfere with.* Even Elly's father seemed unwilling to risk intruding on the brothers' heated debate.

Sucking in a quick breath, Elly stepped between the two men. "Arguing isn't going to do any good," she stated firmly.

They glowered over her head at each other, and she was struck again by the remarkable resemblance between the two men. Couldn't they see it for themselves? They shared a father's blood! Didn't that count for anything?

"Listen," she tried again, "maybe a formal dinner isn't the place for this discussion. It seems to me that you're both saying the same thing—neither of you likes the situation. Your Highness," she said turning to Jacob, "I don't know Daniel Eastwood that well. But it appears to me that he only wants to be left alone. He isn't looking for profit from these unexpected circumstances."

Elly's gaze shifted to Dan. "Put yourself in Jacob's shoes. It's natural for this to be a difficult time for any family. But the von Austerands have a lot to lose if things aren't handled the right way."

"What you mean by *the right way* is that you think the past should be hushed up. I'm not sure that's fair to everyone involved." Dan glanced meaningfully toward his mother.

Madge shook her head nervously. "Please. I don't want a lot of fuss on my account."

"Giving you the credit you're due for having raised a son on your own isn't making a fuss," Frank said in a gentler version of his customary raspy voice.

"You act as if this is my or my mother's fault," Dan growled, his face glowing with fury. He lunged forward, pushing Elly aside to get closer to Jacob.

Immediately, two burly bodyguards moved in from shadowy corners of the room. Jacob waved them off with a look of annoyance.

"Go on," he said. "You might as well get if off your chest."

Elly found herself holding her breath. She forced down a gulp of air and prayed the two of them wouldn't kill each other before the night was through.

Dan faced his brother, matching his aggressive hands-on-hips, chin-shot-up stance. "My mother didn't ask to be burdened with a baby. If there is blame, it should go to your father for deceiving a young girl and leaving her pregnant!"

"I'll thank you not to speak of my father with disrespect when he cannot be here to defend himself!" Jacob snapped.

"The fact that he's *dead* doesn't change what he did!" Dan insisted. "He took advantage of a young woman's innocence. No woman should feel compelled to bear a child she doesn't want."

Elly's heart caught in her throat. Could he possibly realize how closely his statement echoed her own feelings?

Jacob's cold glare shifted subtly to a thin smile. "Interesting," he murmured. "You are arguing against your own existence. But you *do* exist, Mr. Eastwood, and I venture to say that a man in your position, who feels as strongly as you do about a wrong done to someone he loves, will exact a punishment. I know I would." The harsh gleam in Jacob's dark eyes left no doubt about that. "I would want retribution for my mother. *Tell me, sir, that you do not!*"

The tension in the room was as thick as a New England coastal fog. Elly reached out to touch Dan's arm at the same moment Allison rested her fingertips on the king's clenched hand, raised threateningly before him.

"Please," Elly said softly, "let's eat. We're all tired and hungry, and that can't improve our tempers. Later, you two can agree on a more private setting to discuss this."

Allison gave her an appreciative blink of her blue eyes then stated with regal firmness, "I agree. We will have our dinner now, Jacob. Let's give reason a chance to prevail."

Elly waited on pins and needles all the next morning, fearful that one of the brothers had surely murdered the other by then. Except there were those bodyguards, who likely wouldn't stand by while Dan decked Jacob. So she revised her imagination's view of events. Dan was either nursing serious wounds or was chained in the tower. Or both.

Despite its emotional beginning, the meal the previous night had been magnificent—seven courses of heaven. But Elly would have enjoyed it far more without the suffocating tension in the hall. Conversation was kept intentionally light. Nothing more important than plans for cross-country skiing or shopping trips were discussed. The evening ended with an invitation for Dan to meet with Jacob in his private office the following morning. No one else was asked to be present.

At a little after noon, a knock sounded on Elly's door. She dove for it and opened it to find Dan in an agitated state. "He wants me to sign *documents!*" he growled, rushing past her and into the bedchamber.

Elly scowled at him. "Documents? What kind?"

"Legal statements drawn up by his royal lawyers,

saying that I'm not related to him or his family in any way.''

She gasped. ''But that's a lie!''

''Exactly. I told him I wouldn't do it.'' Dan paced the room like a caged beast.

Elly thought for a moment. ''I'm sure Jacob is just trying to find a way to outwit the press. That would be to both your advantages.''

''I know, but I can't do what my mother has done all of these years—deny the past.'' He let out a long groan of exasperation. ''Besides, the woman deserves something for all she went through because of that man.''

''You mean Karl, your father,'' Elly said softly.

''My father!'' He laughed wildly, shaking his head. ''A pompous, spoiled aristocratic teenager, no doubt. Probably spawned dozens of little Karls all over Europe.''

''I don't believe so,'' Elly said, coming to his side. She could feel his hurt, his anger, as if his emotion seeped into her pores from the air between them. But she sensed his turbulent state wasn't all on behalf of Madge. He himself must have felt betrayed. ''I expect your father wanted very much to find you and your mother.''

He rounded on her, eyes ablaze. ''Why? To bribe her to silence?''

''I don't think so,'' Elly said slowly. ''I've read the letters he wrote to her during the years after she left Paris, when he was trying to contact her. They are beautiful, tender love letters, begging her forgiveness, asking her to reveal to him where she had gone so that he could help her.''

''Then he knew of my existence?''

Elly hesitated. "We're not sure. He might have guessed. Madge didn't tell him why she was leaving him, other than to say that she'd discovered his true identity and knew they couldn't remain together."

"The bastard broke her heart!" Dan snapped. As she looked up at him, a blue vein throbbed at his temple. His eyes were hot and glistening with tears he was too proud to shed.

He glared at the stone wall to his right and, for an instant, she could imagine a rage and frustration so great he might throw a fist at the cold, gray marble.

Elly's heart went out to Dan. She stepped in front of him and brought her hands up to frame both sides of his strong jaw. "I know Karl hurt her," she whispered. "It was wrong that he deceived her. But I believe from all I've read of his correspondence that he deeply loved your mother and only wanted to hold on to her for as long as he was able. Eventually, his duty to the crown dictated his marriage to the woman betrothed to him. He had no choice, Dan. Not at that time, before the rules were challenged by his own son, Jacob."

Dan gripped her wrists as if to pull them away from his face, but his eyes met hers and something sharp and quick and piercing passed between them that transcended his bitterness. In a single motion, he stepped forward, backing Elly into the wall. She felt the cool curve of each stone from her hips to her shoulder blades.

Elly knew before his mouth covered hers that he was going to kiss her unless she struggled or cried out for him to release her. And she would do neither because she had wanted him since the moment they had met and now the need had intensified to a white heat that defied common sense as well as her own secret fears.

His hands found their way to her breasts through the bodice of her dress. They kneaded her pliant flesh and raised her nipples to hard peaks that pressed through the fabric. She felt her insides go liquid. A welcome heat pulsed through her body.

He didn't ask her permission. It was as if he understood the surge of desire rushing through her body, which fed his own. His mouth lifted from hers. Gasping for breath she curled her fingers through the short hairs at the nape of his neck and nibbled hungrily at the spot on his throat where the muscles angled along his shoulder.

She luxuriated in the sensation of his hands moving over her, through clothing, then beneath. Her flesh prickled and danced at his touch. She glanced down to see that the buttons at the front of her dress had come open, and she sensed that he was waiting just these few seconds to see if she might protest. When she didn't, he snapped the front clasp of her bra between thumb and finger, and it parted to expose her breasts.

As he bowed to touch a nipple with the tip of his tongue she arched toward him, asking for more. He complied, drawing the soft flesh into his mouth, warming her with his tongue, teasing the erect brown tip with the sharp edges of his teeth. Her fingers bit gloriously into his shoulders, and she dropped her head back against the stone.

He grasped her hand urgently in his. "Touch me."

Unsure of what he wanted at first, she let him guide her hand down the length of his body. Beneath the zipper of his pants she felt his strength, his hardness.

"I know it's too soon," he growled. "But I need you to know how much I want you, Elly."

Too soon? She thought dizzily. *Or has it been far, far too long?*

It seemed as if all of her life she'd waited for a man who could come this close to making her forget all the hurt and loss and heartache of the day she'd lost both mother and infant brother. And the emptiness of her own childless future.

The emotional connection had been there between them from the start, she now realized. She understood his turmoil, believed in him, wanted to comfort him in this difficult time of his life. And maybe she even wanted his strength and comfort for herself. Maybe she could trust him enough to accept those gifts from him. He was right, she reluctantly admitted; they'd known each other only a handful of days. But she pushed that knowledge aside, refusing to let rational thoughts dictate her actions this one time.

Elly kissed Dan with fierce abandon, pressing her hand against his hardness.

He let out a low moan at the parting of their lips. "Don't do that again unless you—" Interrupting him by pressing her mouth over his, she put more pressure behind her hand. He gasped for breath. "—mean it."

She let her lips part, silently inviting him to deepen their kiss. They touched tongues. His hands slid possessively up beneath her skirt. Through the thin silk of her panties, he touched her.

Then the one thing she most dreaded happened.

As if something mechanical inside of her suddenly shut down, she felt nothing where all the warmth had been. Then the nothing turned cold and frightening. Her mother's swollen face flashed before her, then the image of a tiny casket lying beside a larger one. The old terror seized her, turning every sweet impulse into lethal temptation. Elly's body stiffened in Dan's arms.

"What?" he asked.

"I can't," she whispered, the words catching in her throat. Her eyes burned, and she squeezed them closed and wished with all her heart that she could find the strength to give herself to this wonderful man. "I want to, but I can't."

"I can protect you, Elly."

"No. You're right. It's too soon." It would always be too soon for her.

He was silent for a long moment. Then he opened his arms and stepped away from her. The disappointment in his handsome face broke her heart. She'd have given anything to please him and to satisfy the longing within herself.

Elly slumped against the wall, feeling lost, inadequate, chilled.

"Do you want to talk about it?" he asked.

What good would that do? All she could say was what had already been said. She shook her head. "I'm sorry. I wasn't trying to be a tease or lead you on."

"I know," he whispered, touching her cheek with his fingertips. "When the time is right...when the person is right, it will happen."

She gazed up at him desolately. "You really think so?"

He smiled. "I do. I'd just really like that someone to be me, Elly."

Four

As a man accustomed to an active life, Dan had found only two methods of achieving the physical release his body required on a regular basis. The first was by working out, usually by swimming. But lifting weights was acceptable when the weather was so terrible he couldn't bear plunging into frigid water. The other was through sex.

The second was harder to come by because there wasn't always an available partner. And as the years moved along he found himself less and less inclined to be intimate when he didn't feel an emotional as well as a physical connection with a woman. As luck would have it, he'd felt both with Elly, fiercely so. But she hadn't been able to give herself to him, and the frustration he suffered as a result was unnerving.

He didn't blame her at all. He sensed her need was as great as his, if not greater. He felt confident he could help her, if only he could break through the emotional barrier she'd lived behind for so long. How he'd go about that without forcing her, though, he had no idea. And force was definitely out of the question.

Meanwhile, there was the problem of his growing restlessness and hunger for physical action. He missed his early-morning swims, and he thought constantly of Elly, her sweet kisses and lovely breasts. He decided he'd have to settle for a good hard run to work off his body's mounting tension.

He had packed running shorts, a T-shirt, athletic shoes and socks. Even though it was winter and snow from the last storm stood in low heaps throughout the garden and on street corners, most of the streets themselves were bare. Besides, he was accustomed to running barelegged on the beach even during the coldest months. He jogged out through the open gates of the Crystal Palace, giving the guard a wave as he left to make sure the man would recognize him and let him in when he returned.

For the first mile he felt stiff, and every stride required intense labor. His breathing was tight. His pores began to sweat in response to the exertion. Somewhere in the middle of the second mile, the muscles in his thighs and hips loosened, and his arms began to pump smoothly at his sides like well-maintained machine parts. His shoulders and neck felt relaxed. He moved with the automatic grace of an athlete.

Dan looped through the quaint medieval streets of Elbia, the only real city in the tiny country by the same name. If a visitor didn't know better, Dan mused, that person might assume he'd either been transported back in time by hundreds of years, or else this was an immense amusement park that had been built to resemble a historical period. But Elly had told him a little of the amazing history of Elbia, which had survived two modern wars and many ancient ones. As he ran faster, harder, he marveled at colorful shops that might have been kept by the great-grandfathers of present owners, not yet open for the day, and the homes with their sturdy stucco-and-stone walls and charming peaked tile roofs.

He set each foot carefully, stride after long stride, on the rounded cobbles, concentrating on working his body, less and less aware of the carved wooden signs dangling from chains over the sidewalks and the flashes of color from shop windows. It was Elly's sweet face that floated before him. She was a lovely enigma, a challenge and a troubled soul. Yet, as difficult as it was to overcome her fears and win her trust, he sensed the effort would be well worth it to a man. If only he had the patience to hold out that long.

Then a disturbing thought came to him.

She was clearly attracted to him, and they had been well on their way to making love the night before. But why was she so willing to be with him if she was really so terrified of having children and she knew that he wanted them? Was it because she had known from the day she'd waved him down on the beach in Ocean City that he was the son of a king? Because she figured he was marked to inherit thousands, possibly millions?

Even more alarming was his own longing for her despite her having made it clear she would never agree to have children. He felt he was a fair man, willing to make compromises. He no longer expected to find the perfect woman—the ideal blend of intelligence, sexuality, gentleness, beauty and practicality. But the decision to create a family, to have babies or remain childless, was a make-or-break point in the classic bargain struck between a man and a woman, at least as far as he was concerned.

At this time in his life, when he should have been seriously focusing on the woman capable of and willing to be the mother of his children, he should have walked away from Elizabeth Anderson. Instead, he hungered for her.

Feeling more and more off balance, Dan swung back along the outer edges of the city as the streets began to come alive with people opening their shops or seeking their morning coffee and fresh roll before heading for work. The palace gates came into view. Something had changed. He slowed at the unexpected sight before him.

A cluster of men and women armed with cameras, microphones and compact tape recorders slung over shoulders milled around outside the main gate. A man with a TV camera propped on one shoulder was shooting between the iron bars, which had been shut. One guard stood alertly inside the massive metal grille, another outside, watching the cameraman warily.

Dan came to an abrupt stop, hesitated a moment, then slowly approached the group. The outside guard saw him just as Dan was about to raise his hand to signal he had returned. Before he could do or say anything, the soldier broke through the crowd and came swiftly to Dan's side.

"This way, please sir," he said in heavily accented English.

With a hand on Dan's shoulder blade, the guard pushed him between camera-whirring, question-shouting reporters. The other guard already had cracked open the gate. With a sudden lunge Dan and his escort were through it and into the safety of the courtyard. The disappointed paparazzi were left outside, still shouting, clicking and whirring.

"What the hell is going on?" Dan gasped for breath.

"We were hoping, sir, that you would return before they arrived."

"You knew this would happen?"

"It wasn't unexpected, sir."

Dan shook his head and allowed them to usher him through the towering central doors into the great hall where Jacob stood between Elly and his queen. All three turned toward him with worried expressions. Jacob's bloomed into anger at the sight of his half brother.

"*Where* have you been?" Elly asked breathlessly.

Dan shrugged. "Out for a run. Is that a crime in this country?"

Jacob took a step forward, glowering at him. "It was a foolish thing to do. We might have found a way to send them away if they hadn't seen you. Now there is no hope of denying your presence in Elbia."

"I came here to work out a solution to this mess," Dan growled. "I'm not hiding from anyone."

"Not very well you're not!" Jacob snapped.

Elly stepped between the two men. "This isn't helping. Stop arguing, please."

The young king stared coldly at her as if shocked by her continued interruptions. Elly felt chilly sweat rise across the nape of her neck. What had she been thinking, talking to him that way? If Jacob sent her away, she'd be unable to right their mistakes and rebuild her father's company's reputation. Then there came an even darker thought: *She'd never see Daniel Eastwood again.*

Allison sighed. "Jacob, please, she's only trying to help. And your brother doesn't yet understand how it is here...how we must live in the public eye." She smiled adoringly at him, and Jacob visibly relaxed a notch.

"I'm beginning to get the idea," Dan muttered, "and I can't say that I like it. I needed to work out. You don't seem to have a convenient ocean, so I thought a run through—"

"In the first level below ground, there is a gymnasium with every sort of equipment you might require," Jacob said. "All you had to do was ask."

Dan observed him, trying to figure out what made the two of them go at each other's throats this way whenever they were in the same room. Did all brothers do this at one time or another? Battling like two male lions competing for dominance in the pride? Maybe because they had grown up apart, not meeting until they were adults, they had to fight their way through this stage of their relationship now? Whatever the reason, he resented Jacob for interfering in his life and for ordering him around.

"Don't you ever feel you just have to break free, Your Highness?" Dan asked in a low voice. "Don't you ever yearn to get the hell out of these stone walls?"

For a long moment, Jacob just stared at him, and neither woman dared speak. Then Jacob's lips barely moved. "Nearly every day of my life. *Nearly every day.*"

Dan was stunned. His brother was human after all, and perhaps more like him than either of them had guessed.

Allison's hand reached out and touched her husband's arm. She turned to smile faintly at Dan. "We both look forward to the quiet days when the international press corps is off covering other people's lives in other countries. That happens so seldom. We rarely can travel outside Elbia without at least a small contingent of reporters."

Dan met Jacob's eyes. There was no softening in them, but there was a flash of longing for solitude and peace that he could understand only too well. If they had just been two ordinary guys back in Ocean City, Jacob would match him stroke by stroke in the chilly Atlantic along a deserted beach at dawn. But here in his royal world he would never know the luxury of privacy.

"I'm sorry if I've caused a stir," Dan said sincerely. "I didn't mean to."

Jacob gave him a brief nod of acknowledgment. "What's done is done." He started to turn away. "Let's adjourn to my office. My PR officer is meeting us there, and we can discuss a statement to placate the press."

Dan looked down at his sweaty T-shirt and brought the bottom edge up to wipe the sweat from his face. "I'd like to change first, if that's all right."

"Certainly," Jacob said.

Dan started toward the stairs leading to the upper chambers, but Jacob called after him. "I should mention that I've conferred with my advisors, and I can offer you a monetary settlement for publicly renouncing the throne. Since lying to the public is something you disdain, this will enable you still to claim my father as yours, but will get you off the hook since you say you don't want anything to do with the von Austerands and Elbia. You can sign the agreement today if you like.''

Dan froze, mid step. He turned and looked at Elly, whose face had turned ashen, as if she knew what his reaction would be before he did. She blinked once at him, urging caution and restraint, he supposed.

But he wasn't in the mood for tiptoeing around issues or for doing something just because it was a convenient solution for his brother. He rounded slowly to face Jacob across the expanse of pale gray marble, his hand gripping the carved banister.

"Listen," he said slowly, "I may be just a city kid who fought his way to making good in a small way. I may not live in a castle or have a title or be able to live in your grand manner, Jacob. But I am proud of who I am. Not because I have a king's blood in me. Just because I'm me.''

Jacob's eyes darkened to blue-black chips of obsidian, but he said nothing.

"I resent you treating me like an intruder and trying to buy me off.'' Dan paused long enough to let his last words sink in and make sure Jacob was listening to the rest. "I won't sign your document or accept a penny from you.''

Less than an hour later, Dan stood at a casement window, his mood still dark as he looked over the formal gardens behind the castle. Paths looped through dormant winter shrubs as dusk fell. Nearly hidden by tall evergreen hedges was a glass-walled gazebo. Still within the castle walls but barely visible from where he stood was the helicopter pad where they'd landed earlier that day.

He pinched the bridge of his nose between thumb

and forefinger, trying to erase the growing tension he felt in a tight band across his forehead. He was worried about a lot of things, including the incident in Elly's room. The memory of their embrace still erupted in little simmering pools of heat in unexpected places within his body.

But now he thought again about Madge. She seemed to blame herself for the current complications in his life. Although they'd initially arrived in the royal city without fanfare or any sign of reporters, it had been only a very short while before the press figured out where their quarry was hiding. Since then his mother had appeared more and more nervous.

Dan didn't understand all this fuss over a love affair that had ended decades ago, but Elly assured him the public's interest would be high enough to spur on greedy tabloid stringers and photo jocks. For now, though, the castle seemed a peaceful enough place. He stared down at the rose bushes, dormant for the winter, and imagined how beautiful they would be in full bloom, come the spring. And the snow-covered mountains hovering behind a purplish haze in the distance…how magnificent this land and this immense structure that surrounded him were! It was hard to believe a castle had been his father's home, which made the place Dan's own ancestral home. That would take some getting used to.

"What are you thinking?"

He turned at the gentle sound of Elly's voice. "About destiny, I suppose."

"Destiny?" She pursed her lips and frowned. "Why is that?"

"I look around this amazing place where I've never been. Yet somehow it feels familiar to me." He wiggled an eyebrow at her, going for a lighter tone than he felt. "Spooky, huh?"

"Definitely." She came up beside him and peered through the narrow opening in the stone wall.

The glass pane had an antique, wavy appearance that made it appear he was viewing the world through water. At the time the palace had been built, he supposed, there must have been no glass at all to cover windows, then the place would have been very drafty indeed. Centuries had seen the structure modernized—electricity installed in the main wings, plumbing added. But it still felt richly gripped by the past.

He thought about his father, whom he'd never met, standing on this very spot. And his grandfather...then the men of his family for many generations before.

"You said the von Austerands have been in power for five hundred years?"

"About," she said. "They wrestled this tiny kingdom from the Holy Roman Empire back in the sixteenth century. Somehow they've managed to hold on to it through wars and power struggles."

"Amazing," he breathed, "to be part of that."

"Yes." She looked up at him with shining eyes.

Later, he was never quite sure what came over him at that moment. Perhaps it was merely the romantic influence of history, or the idea of being a healthy male descended from a long line of conquerors. It was true that Elly was gazing up at him as if he really was the prince they claimed him to be. For whatever the reason, history or hormones, he felt compelled to conquer her.

She was so close to him already that all he had to do was drop an arm around her waist and curl her into his chest. Her sultry hazel eyes flashed at him, her lips parting in surprise. He quickly bent down to touch his mouth to hers. Her lips quivered then tensed. He lightly teased them to life again with his own.

When he lifted his head, she rested her cheek against his chest. "I thought we weren't going to do this."

"That was your decision. Let's just say, as much as I'd like to honor your wishes, milady, I'm having a real hard time keeping my distance."

She said nothing.

"Elly, maybe now isn't the time, with all that's going on and understanding as I do that you have issues of your own to deal with. But I just want you to know, I'd give half my kingdom to sleep with you."

She laughed at him and shook her head. "You don't have a kingdom to give away, unless you count the Haven. Anyway, I wouldn't talk like that in front of Jacob or anyone in his court. They'll think you're out to overthrow the crown."

"I wouldn't want the job if they offered it," he stated, touching the soft curls framing her face. They looked like burnished copper in the late-afternoon light. The strands felt warm to his touch. "I like my life the way it is…with one exception. Children. And one special woman to make them with." And it would be nice, awfully nice, if she could be as pretty and warm and appealing as Elizabeth Anderson, he mused.

Elly shivered in his arms as if she'd heard his thoughts.

"Why are you so uncomfortable with any mention of my wanting a family?"

"You know why," she said tightly.

"Two people don't have to choose names for their offspring just because they've kissed once or twice."

"Of course not," she agreed with a nervous laugh. But her pretty eyes skittered away from his.

"And we wouldn't have to reserve a church if I were to touch you like this." He curved his palm around her cheek, then let it drift down her flushed throat to rest just above her breast.

"Absolutely not," she murmured huskily, bringing her glance back to his with steamy intensity.

Dan subconsciously listened for footsteps down the corridors. None echoed against the stone.

He lowered his head slowly and touched his lips to hers again, deepening the kiss, tasting her honeyed mouth, trying not to think too hard about where this delicious moment might be headed. Or how soon she would stop him. When he stroked the back of his fingers down the side of her breast she lifted her arms around his neck, and he hoped against hope that she wouldn't make him release her this time.

"We want different things," she whispered.

"Do we really?" he asked, observing her with a tense smile. "Right now, there's only one that comes to mind."

"I don't mean *that*. I mean, the desired result is different. You want a family, I don't."

He moved her back from him just the few inches necessary to study her expression. "Two things, woman," he said. "First, this is the twenty-first century. We have something called birth control. Two people can sleep together without getting pregnant." He tapped a finger over her lips when she started to protest. "Secondly, maybe I don't consider you wife-and-mother material. Ever thought of that, sweet Elly? Maybe I just want to roll around with you on that big, canopied bed in my suite because you're a beautiful woman who turns me on. End of story."

She stared up at him, a frown furrowing her brow.

He didn't know if she believed him or even if he believed himself. What did it matter? He wanted to touch every imaginable spot on her body. If nothing but pure pleasure came of their intimacy, then that might not be such a terrible thing. It had been a long time since a woman had moved him this way. In fact, he couldn't recall when, if ever, that time had been.

"I've only known you for a few days," she murmured. "I don't sleep with strangers or—"

He pressed his lips over hers, refusing to hear generic objections. If she was going to turn him down, she'd have to do it honestly. "Just tell me you don't want to sleep with me," he said as his mouth left hers. "I'll never bring it up again."

"Liar."

"Try me."

She was silent in his arms. He smiled. Good.

At last she spoke carefully. "I'm not saying that you don't get me a little—" she hesitated "—a little *provoked* in a rather enjoyable way. I just don't want to rush into anything and disappoint either of us."

He put on a wounded expression for her. "You think you'd be disappointed after making love with me?" He caressed her throat then drew his fingertips slowly down her shoulder, along her arm, until they finally wove between hers.

She shivered, looking confused. "That's not what I meant. I just wouldn't want to hurt you, Dan, if things got serious."

"Why don't you let me worry about that? I'm pretty good at taking care of myself. If growing up in Baltimore didn't teach me that, the marines sure did."

Elly blinked up at him, and all she could think was, *But what about me? Who is going to take care of me when I can't live up to what you want?* Because Daniel Eastwood, despite his flirting and insistence that he was just interested in a good time, was ultimately a man who would find one woman to marry and have kids with. Probably lots of them. And when he found that woman, none of his lovers before her would matter. Including Elizabeth Anderson.

The realization sent an oppressive wave of sadness over her. To be able to be that woman would be wonderful. But it was her fate to be the woman left behind, for she could never give him a child, or at least be sure that she would be there to raise their baby with him. Aside from her own physical impairment and fear of death, she couldn't bear the thought of causing any man she cared for the grief her father had suffered.

"It's better that we not get involved," she said hastily, then desperately searched for excuses. She could only come up with a lame, "You know, with all that's going to be happening in the next few weeks."

The earthy brown of his eyes intensified, and she saw something in them she hadn't noticed before and couldn't define. Determination? Patience? Or just pure stubbornness? Was he reacting to her refusal as if it was a challenge? By telling him they couldn't possibly become involved, while letting him know that she was tempted, had she inadvertently waved a red flag before the man?

"Really," she whispered, moving herself out of his arms, "it's much better if we keep this on a professional level."

Elly stood outside the door to Dan's chamber in the castle the next day and knocked a third time. There was no answer. Something told her that he wasn't inside ignoring her. The room behind the closed door felt empty.

She felt awful for putting Dan through so much. By bringing him to Elbia Elly had meant to make things easier for everyone. But now everything seemed worse. More confusing, more complex than ever. There was so much to settle between Jacob and Dan...and so much to untangle between Dan and herself. For although she'd tried to return their relationship to one based purely on her professional capacity, she wasn't convinced that was possible. Not when he looked at her the way he did.

Now she tried to think where he might have gone. He would naturally seek water, a beach, when he was troubled and felt trapped. Probably the Adriatic was closest. But that was hundreds of miles away.

If not an ocean, then at least the out-of-doors, and that could only mean the garden since Jacob had ordered all of them to remain within the castle grounds until further notice.

Stopping at her own room only long enough to grab her coat, she ran through soaring stone hallways of an ancient wing of the castle lit by amber electric sconces and down a rear stairwell to a door she hoped would bring her directly into the gardens. There was one at last, of heavy oak studded with iron bolts. A modern deadbolt had replaced whatever older latch had been there, and she turned the lock then tugged on the weighty door. It creaked open and sunlight poured through, forcing her to squint into its winter brilliance.

Stepping outside, she shaded her face with one hand and gave her eyes a chance to adjust to the sun. She breathed in air scented with mountains, pine and an astonishing absence of petroleum residue. Although cars were not banned in Elbia, it was easy to get around the city and countryside by bicycle or on the little red buses that cheerfully plied the hilly streets, and few residents bothered with the expense of buying an automobile.

She walked down a brick path through the rose garden. The bushes were little more than dry sticks, neatly pruned to encourage a fresh burst of flowers come warm weather. Further on was a formal English-style garden of hedges, smartly clipped to resemble whimsical creatures and clever geometric designs. She went on and came to another area where a gazebo grown over with ivy sat at the center of converging paths. A shadow moved behind frosty panes of glass. Cautiously, she approached, still unable to make out who might be inside.

When she was only a few feet from the door, the figure turned as if it had seen her. She froze, not daring to come closer. It was Dan, she was sure of it. The width of his shoulders and dark hair could only have belonged to one of the two brothers. And she remembered Dan had been wearing a deep blue shirt. He opened the door for her.

"Join me?" he said, stepping aside to let her in.

She climbed the steps and moved past him as he shut the door behind them. It was still cold but being out of the wind helped. The sun shining through the glass provided natural solar warmth.

Elly took her hands out of her coat pockets and rubbed them together as she studied his expression. "Are you all right?"

"Of course I'm all right," he muttered irritably. "Why shouldn't I be?"

"That was quite a scene between you and Jacob yesterday. And then, there's been the stuff happening between us. I hope I haven't hurt your feelings.''

''I don't know what he expects,'' Dan mumbled, ignoring the second part of her statement as he scraped the sole of one shoe against the dark green floor boards. ''No, I take that back. I do know all too well what he expects.'' He narrowed his eyes and glared at her. ''Jacob believes he can have everything his way, because that's how it's always been for him.''

Elly decided maybe Dan's tactic was best. They would simply ignore their attraction and address other issues. She shook her head. ''I don't think so. He may come off as arrogant and stubborn, but he's not an unreasonable man. My dad and I talked with him after you left yesterday. He desperately wants to protect his people and his crown, but he also wants to find a way to do the right thing by you and Madge. This isn't your average family, you know. Things become a bit more complicated when you're sovereign over a country.'' She tried out a weak smile on him.

''Right,'' he agreed dryly.

Elly stepped closer, feeling an energy between them dragging her even nearer. We're the moon and the tide, she thought. She resisted but only with great effort.

''Look,'' she whispered, ''I know you have your pride. But don't punish your mother because of it. And don't be blind to all the good that can come of this.''

''*What* good?'' he snapped.

She sighed. Why was it so difficult for men to accept a gift without attaching an ulterior motive to it? ''What if you accept Jacob's settlement on behalf of your City Kids beach program? Let your mom do what she wishes with her share. Or, if she won't take it, invest it for her so that if she ever needs the money for medical care or assisted-living arrangements, she'll have it.''

He glared at the toes of his shoes but said nothing.

She continued quickly, gratified that he was, at least, listening to her. ''You don't have to take a penny for yourself, Dan. But those kids you care so much about…they could really benefit. How many more of them each summer could you bring to Ocean City with Jacob's help? What about constructing extra lodging space near the Haven? Or a special educational center where your campers could experiment with computers or learn technical skills that might help them get jobs some day? The possibilities for good are endless with enough funds.''

Dan lifted troubled eyes to her face. ''I'll think about it.''

''Promise?''

''Promise.'' He lifted one corner of his lips in a half smile.

She sensed that he meant it, that he'd gotten her message. But the way his eyes had deepened to a richer color and seemed suddenly alive with hot sparks also told her that he had put aside questions of pride, money and summer camp for considerations of a much more elemental nature. Elly's heartbeat quickened. Suddenly she found breathing a struggle.

''Wh-what are you thinking?'' she stammered.

He tipped his head to one side and focused on her all the more closely. ''That you feel as deeply about children as I do, only you try not to show it.''

She swallowed. ''I just hate to see great opportunities go to waste.''

''No, it's more than that.'' His gaze was crisply perceptive. He stepped up to her. ''You want kids of your

own, don't you? Deep down, I mean, beyond all the
fear and sad memories, you *want* them.''

A solid knot grew in her throat. The beginnings of
tears prickled behind her lashes. "We can't have everything we want. Sometimes we just have to settle for
what's best for us...what's safe.''

"So there *are* regrets," he said, hitting too close to
home. "How will you deal with those regrets later on,
Elly? What happens when you are forty years old, fifty
or sixty, and your dad is gone and it's just you? Will
you look back on these barren years and be content?
Or will you ache for the children and grandchildren
other women have?''

She turned sharply away from him and blinked back
fat tears. "Stop that! Not everyone is meant to be a
parent. I *like* my independence. I enjoy being—'' How
was she ever going to finish that sentence? *Alone?* I
like being *alone?* That wasn't true. As a child she had
thrived on being part of a family. She would have welcomed two, three, six brothers and sisters, if only she
could have kept her mother too.

"You like being what, Elly?'' He moved to within
inches of her, and she jerked backward but had nowhere to go. The glass walls of the gazebo curved
around behind her.

"I like...not having to *worry* about other people,''
she blurted out. "With children, I'd be fussing over
them all the time, afraid they'd be struck down by dis-
ease, hit by a car or beaten up by school bullies. I'd
be a *horrible* mother.''

His hand lifted to twist a strand of her red hair. "I
think you'd make a wonderful mother. There are, you
know, no guarantees in life. Whenever we want something that's very important to us, we must give up

something in return. And when things don't work out as we wish, we have to go on with life.''

Elly's lips trembled. Tears spilled down her cheeks, but she dashed them away with the back of her hand. ''Don't do this to me, Dan. Don't make me feel selfish.''

''That's not what I want you to feel.''

She choked on a sob. ''What then?''

He moved forward and took her in his arms. The warmth was incredible. ''I just want you to be sure of what you really want or don't want. Regret is the bitterest of pills.''

She swallowed, staring helplessly up at him as he held her. ''I've often wondered if she knew.''

''She?'' He looked confused.

''My mother. I've tried putting myself in her place. I wonder if she understood the risks of her heart condition, if she'd been warned by her doctor that even a C-section would be dangerous, but she never said anything about it to me...maybe not even to my father. She wanted a second baby so badly, but for a long time she just couldn't seem to get pregnant again. Then several years passed and my parents stopped talking about another child.''

''They'd given up?'' he guessed.

''Or maybe that was when the doctor told her that it would be too risky to try again,'' she whispered against his chest. Why was it so much easier to speak of these things, these terribly sad things, while Dan was holding her like this? ''I just miss her so very much.''

It was impossible to stop crying now. Elly wept openly and Dan held her, letting her mourn the woman who had brought her into the world, allowing her to cleanse her heart of the bitterness and grief that kept her from loving fully and openly. He didn't try to stop her tears, didn't tell her that everything would be all right or that she would forget her mother's sacrifice. And she silently thanked him for that small, precious gift of silence, of compassion.

When the tears finally stopped, Elly felt lighter of spirit.

Dan didn't speak now. He just ran the pad of his wide thumb beneath each of her eyes in turn, wiping away the moisture as she gazed up at him. He wasn't smiling and he wasn't frowning. His expression was one of concentration on an important task. So she didn't see the kiss coming until his mouth had pressed gently but firmly over hers.

She savored the melting sensation of their lips. Emotions burst from her as if reborn from within a dead soul. A whirl of feelings wrapped around her—so heady, so potent that her knees almost buckled beneath her.

As if knowing this, Dan tightened his arms around her, supporting her against his body as his kiss deepened. The world spun. The gazebo's windows swam before her eyes, glittering in winter sunlight. The air felt suddenly thinner, finer, easier to breathe and she was no longer aware of chill beyond the warm circle of Dan's arms. The darkness of the past receded.

Elly's breasts pressed against the curve of his muscled abdomen. She could feel each ridge, each toned band made taut by miles of swimming. Her jacket had fallen open, and he wore no coat. She was sure he was as aware of her body as she was of his. It seemed as if they'd escaped to a world of their own—apart from family, the castle's immense staff, the press who would continue to hound Dan now that they'd found him.

He had spoken to her heart, and his words might not solve all of her problems, but they had healed a small part of her and brought new hope to her life. He was right, of course. She wasn't guaranteeing herself a long, healthy life by avoiding the single potential danger of childbirth. She was simply avoiding life at its richest. And one day, very likely, she would regret her decision. But in the meantime, it was all she could do to consider being close to a man whose masculinity she could even now feel pulsing between them.

Elly kissed him back, deeply, allowing her lips to part welcomingly for him. A small sigh of contentment escaped from her soul. Clinging to him she delighted in the way his hands smoothed upward along her ribs beneath her jacket. His palms pressed against the sides of her breasts through her clothing, and her nipples tingled in anticipation.

It had been so long, so very long since she'd felt desire for a man's touch. And now it seemed as if no man would do but this one. Daniel Eastwood. No less than a prince.

The fierce passion in his eyes told her that he was no longer thinking of anything but the signals their bodies were sending each other. A longing filled Elly to feel him inside her, even if only this one time. The need crowded out all caution, all warnings of consequences.

Dan drew her along with him as he backed up, then sat on a wooden bench. Pulling her down onto his lap he pressed his cheek against the V of her blouse collar then turned his head to kiss the sensitive valley between her breasts.

Elly sucked in a ragged breath, let her head drop back and soaked up every delicious sensation as his lips slipped lower. With one thumb he hooked a bra cup, tugging it down to expose her breast. Cool air tingled against her exposed flesh. He ran the pad of one finger around then across her nipple, and she thought she'd rocket through the glass roof.

"Oh!" She gulped to catch her breath. "Oh, Dan!"

When his mouth closed over her nipple and ravenously feasted, Elly felt a sudden rush of heat between her thighs. She lifted off his lap with a soft gasp of pleasure. His hand took advantage of the new opening and slid between her legs, smoothing upward but stopping short of touching her where the heat had centered most torridly.

She silently begged him not to stop, wanted to ask him to use his strong fingers to stroke and probe her, prolonging the fire building within her body. But she couldn't put her needs into words. And unless she could give him what he wanted in return, she believed it wasn't right to accept the intimacy he was offering her.

Her head fell forward against his strong shoulder and she pressed one palm gently, reluctantly against his chest in a Stop signal. His hand immediately moved back down to neutral territory on her knee. His lips released her breast and he looked questioningly up at her.

"I won't hurt you," he whispered. "I won't let anything happen to you, Elly. Trust me."

With all her heart she wanted to. Her body's hunger called out for him, but the past inevitably crept in over the warmth and desire again. She squeezed her eyes shut.

"I'm sorry…so very sorry," she murmured.

"Sh-sh-sh," he said, soothingly. "It's all right."

It wasn't all right, not by a long shot, she thought. "I can't keep letting things get out of control. I swear, I'm not trying to torment you, Dan. It's just that...that..." She lost it then and broke into tears. "It's just so hard."

"I know," he whispered, holding her, rocking her as his hand stroked the back of her head.

Elly knew he couldn't possibly understand the war being waged inside her between her natural passion and her fears. She hardly understood it herself.

He held her tighter, touching his lips to her damp cheek, bathing it in comforting warmth that never seemed to sink into the rest of her. "It's not important. You're safe with me, Elly. We won't do this again. It's not worth putting you through the agony."

She felt her body finally relax against his, sheltered in his arms.

He spoke softly to her. "If that's what you want, we'll just be friends. Okay?"

It wasn't what she wanted, but it was what she supposed she must settle for. "Okay," she agreed, lapsing into post-sob hiccups. Then she did feel safe, more so than ever in her life.

Five

___

Friends, Dan thought bitterly each day whenever he saw Elly. It wasn't at all what he had wanted, and he didn't know if he could be only that to her. Being holed up in the castle with her made it all the more difficult, for there was no place to escape to.

Ten days after they had arrived in Elbia, neither his relationship with Elly nor the one with Jacob looked any better. Elly kept her distance, and Jacob barely offered him a nod when they happened to pass in a hallway. Dan was pretty sure his brother was avoiding both him and Madge at mealtimes. They'd met formally two more times, but Dan still refused to sign anything, as he remained uncertain that he should be the one to make a decision for his mother. Madge still insisted that she wanted nothing from Karl's estate.

He thought he understood her reluctance to make her liaison with the monarch official. After all, once it was

put in writing that Dan was Karl von Austerand's illegitimate son, Madge's indiscretion would be there for
all the world to see and comment on. And he knew
how much that would hurt her. Then there was the
notoriety that the scandal would bring to the Haven.
He was torn, wishing he knew what was best for everyone.

A good part of the reason he felt unable to think
clearly was Elly. He believed that she felt something
special for him, and that she wanted him as much as
he wanted her. It frustrated him to no end that he'd
promised to stop pursuing her—but what else could he
have done when she obviously was in such pain whenever they came close to intimacy?

Every time he saw her it became more and more a
test of his will not to touch her. The temptation was
nearly impossible to ignore. He began to wonder if his
imagination was playing tricks on him. How could she
have felt so very different in his arms than any other
woman? How could the simple appearance of the
woman in a room send his heart reeling and his libido
into overdrive?

The castle, as immense as it was, no longer felt big
enough to contain the two of them. He grew frantic to
break free—to swim, to run up mountainsides and
down into valleys, to expend some of the pent-up energy being shut up with Elly had built inside him. But
Jacob was insistent that no one leave the castle
grounds, and as much as he hated giving in to his
brother's rules, he supposed they had little alternative.

One morning, ten days after they'd arrived in Elbia,
Dan spent two hours in Jacob's gym, running on the
treadmill then lifting weights. No matter what he did,
he couldn't exhaust himself or stop thinking about Elly.

Then she walked into the gym dressed in hot-pink biking shorts and a matching sports bra—and he rolled his eyes in desperation as his body reacted to her sexy outfit.

"Mind if I join you?" she asked pertly. "I'm going stir crazy."

"Like everyone else in this damn castle," he muttered. "I don't understand the point of this siege mentality. We can't avoid the press forever. What are we waiting for?"

"Jacob's advisors are hoping the paparazzi's fascination with you and Madge will wear out if we're patient enough."

He shook his head. "I wonder..."

Dan lifted a forty-pound dumbbell from the rack and curled it with one hand for another ten repetitions. He watched his biceps swell then relax with each flexing of his arm, but he wasn't paying much attention to the exercise. His mind was on Elly. She looked adorable in her workout gear, so close in design and coverage to underwear. He remembered with intense clarity touching her breasts, now so sparsely covered. He remembered kissing them. A lick of flame swept through him, and he had to put down the dumbbell and take a steadying breath.

"Try to be patient," Elly said encouragingly. "Not even the staff can leave the castle grounds without being accosted by a dozen reporters. We might as well enjoy our captivity in luxury." She smiled at him, as if to gently chide him for his complaints.

He shrugged good-naturedly. "I guess this isn't exactly on a level with being thrown into the dungeon."

"Hardly. Which is another reason why I have to exercise. I've never eaten such amazing food. It's just too delicious to turn down.'' Elly blinked up at him as she strode over to a stationary bicycle and climbed on. ''I stooped to seconds last night,'' she confessed. ''And did you have any of that yummy chocolate torte?''

He shook his head. ''I don't have the sweet tooth you seem to have.'' But he could certainly do with a nibble on her throat right now, he thought without a trace of guilt. Dan slung a towel around his neck and leaned against a wall as he watched her start to pedal.

''Are you finished with your workout?'' she asked.

''I suppose. Don't feel a whole lot better for it. I need to get outside…and I don't mean for a stroll in the garden.'' A thought suddenly struck him. ''You said the staff can't get out without being harassed?''

''That's right. One of the groundskeepers told me that every time he comes or leaves, he's bombarded with questions.'' She laughed. ''He just tells the reporters he never sees any of us, doesn't know a thing.''

''But he comes and goes,'' Dan repeated.

''Well, yes, he has a family in the town and needs to get home to them. But if it were you or me—''

''But that's just the point!'' Dan interrupted her, his spirits soaring at an idea. ''The paparazzi are only interested in the royals, me or Madge…or anyone who is willing to talk about what's happening inside the castle. If a gardener or maid or cook doesn't have information they can use, they don't care how many times they come and go from the castle.''

Elly squinted at him suspiciously. ''So?''

''So maybe another groundskeeper will leave by the back gate this afternoon.''

Understanding brightened her face. ''Dan, you wouldn't…''

"Want to come along?" He sensed, even as he said the words that he was inviting trouble.

Elly laughed. "There's absolutely no way both of us could slip out unnoticed."

"Not exactly unnoticed. Would you prefer to be a cook or a maid?"

She gave him a skeptical smile, but he could tell she was as excited as he was at the prospect of escaping, if only for a short while, from their confinement. "I'll go talk to the cook. She seems a cheery soul. Maybe she'll lend me something from one of her assistants."

Less than an hour later, Elly met Dan inside the door that led from the kitchen on the ground floor out into the gardens.

"Now, you do keep your head down and don't speak a word *auf englisch* while they're in hearing," Cook advised Elly as she helped her on with a white kitchen smock. "You just keep saying, *'Entschuldigung! Ich wisse nichts.'*"

"That means, Excuse me! I know nothing," Elly explained to Dan.

"What about me?" Dan asked. He had already borrowed some old clothing from Cook's husband, the royal family's head gardener.

"Let the *Fraulein* do the talking," Cook said bluntly. "Your *Deutsch ist* lousy."

Dan laughed, not taking offense. "I don't care as long as I get to see something outside of these stone walls."

"Here," Cook said, pressing a mesh shopping bag stuffed with paper-wrapped parcels on Dan, "you may get hungry. I've sent word to the guards on the rear gate that you'll be coming. They will let you out and watch for your return."

"Thank you," Elly said gratefully. "You've been great. You won't get into trouble for helping us, will you?"

Cook winked at her. "The king, he used to lick my cooking spoons as a little boy. He would never be angry with his *Tante* Anna."

As they approached the back gate, Dan felt the tension building in his shoulders and neck. It was so warm that they really didn't need coats, yet their simple locally made garments made them look their parts as a groundsman and cook's assistant.

There seemed to be just as many reporters attached to the rear gate as there had been at the main entrance. As soon as the guard let them through the iron grille a flurry of excitement ran through their ranks. Several started barking into cell phones, alerting others that prey was afoot.

But Elly played her role impeccably. Murmuring a few guttural words in German as Cook had instructed she jutted out her chin, dropped her glance and headed down the road in a stiff stride, all business. Dan stayed close by her side, glowering at the reporters who tossed out hopeful questions. He pulled his cap lower over his eyes and tried to look as bored and unintelligent as possible.

By the time they'd gone a hundred yards down the road, their followers had dismissed them as unlikely sources of information and returned to their positions outside the gates.

Elly laughed out loud as soon as they were out of hearing. "We did it! We actually fooled them!"

"You should take all the credit. If I'd opened my

mouth they would have known immediately that I was an American.'' He looked appreciatively at her. She was glowing, and he felt a shared enthusiasm for the day that spread out before them.

The weather was balmy for winter. The sun shone brightly, chasing away the chill and melting the last traces of snow that lingered among the roots of road-side shrubs.

"I feel positively giddy with freedom!" she cried. "Where will we go? What will we do? How about a stroll around the city?" Her eyes sparkled.

Dan grimaced. "I'm afraid that would increase our chances of being caught. Someone in town will know we're not really from the castle staff."

She stopped walking and frowned. "What then?"

"The lake," he said. "I could see a corner of it from my window, and it doesn't look as if it's that far. A mile or so."

"Good. By the time we get there, I'll be hungry enough for lunch, and we can see what Cook has packed for us." She peered curiously at the mesh bag.

Dan set a crisp walking pace, and Elly seemed to have no trouble keeping up. Color filled her cheeks as they strode away from town, past cottages and into a wooded area that reminded him of tales from his child-hood—Little Red Riding Hood, Hansel and Gretel. He felt free and young and daring, and having Elly at his side made the outing even more delicious.

The knowledge that nothing could happen between them seemed less painful here. They could be friends, as she wanted, and share an outing without feeling compelled to be anything more. He felt in a very rea-sonable, mature mood at the moment.

By the time the trees opened out into a clearing and

he could see a ribbon of blue water before them, his body felt energized from the exercise. He was pleasantly aware of Elly's slim figure beside him, and of her breathing which was quicker and deeper from the walking. But he felt satisfied that he could enjoy her presence without becoming aroused. This is good, he thought.

"Hungry?" she asked.

"If you are, we can eat first."

"First?" She looked around as if trying to assess alternatives, given the deserted woods surrounding them. A worry line creased her forehead.

"I thought we might go for a swim," he suggested.

"You're kidding, in the middle of winter?" She laughed, then went on before he could respond. "Oh, I forgot, you're the one with the elevated body temperature who swims in oceans in November."

He grinned. "Feel this." He took her hand and walked her down to the edge of the water.

She humored him and bent down to touch her fingertips to the water's softly lapping wavelets. Her expression changed from wariness to amazement. "It's warm. Why?"

"Fed by a thermal spring. Cook's husband told me about it while he was dressing me. It stays the same temperature year round." And with the sun beaming down on them, it didn't seem too cold to shed clothing that now felt much too heavy for the day.

"I can't swim very well," Elly objected. "And I don't have a bathing suit."

He winked at her. "You have a natural one."

"Oh, no!" She laughed at him. "Skinny dipping alone might be one thing but not—"

"Not with me looking on with lust in my heart?" he teased her.

"Something like that." Her pretty eyes skittered away from his.

"You wore that stretchy little athletic bra and bike shorts this morning. Didn't cover anything more than undies. Swim in your underwear."

She gazed longingly out over the crystal-blue water. "It does look refreshing," she admitted, "after all that exercise."

"Go for it," he encouraged her, already shrugging out of his jacket and starting to unbutton the gardener's flannel shirt. He stripped down to his hip-hugging briefs.

Elly hesitated only a moment longer. Then, with one final cautious look around her, as if to make sure no one was watching, she tore off her coat then the white cotton smock. She still looked a little nervous, but her eyes gleamed at the water and she ran barefoot toward it shouting at him, "I'll beat you in!"

"Oh no you won't!" he yelled, even as he raced toward the water's edge, flashed past her and dove, slicing through the mirror surface at a shallow angle. The water glided over his flesh, supporting him with less buoyancy than his lady the ocean but still gently lifting him so that he could skim up to the surface with little effort. He broke through with a splash and stood on the silty bottom, looking around for Elly.

She had walked in and stood with the water up to her waist. "This is marvelous! It felt cool near the edge, but there's a current of warmth right where I'm standing. Must be from the spring."

He nodded, pretending to listen to her words, but far more interested in the view—her pert breasts rising seductively above her bra, her slim waist, her eyes shining at him.

"Could you swim well enough to make it up the shore to that floating log?" he asked, pointing a hundred feet or so up the beach.

"Probably. I can manage a decent doggie paddle," she admitted, "and a slow crawl. I took summer swimming classes at the Y when I was a teenager."

"Let's go then." He started out slowly, giving her time to get used to the feel of the water around her body, then he let her set the pace. She had a nice, compact stroke, although he suspected she'd tire quickly, not being used to swimming any distance or often. He liked the way she seemed to feel comfortable in the water, turning her face into it for two good strokes before swiveling her head to the right for a breath.

They reversed direction and came back to where they had started. When she stood up, Elly looked toward the woods.

"Still worried about Peeping Toms?" he teased.

"I thought I saw something move near those trees."

Dan looked but could see nothing. He came behind her, wrapped his arms around her and gave her a quick, reassuring hug. When she lifted her head he gave her a light kiss on the lips over her shoulder, then quickly backed off. "More likely a deer or a fox than a person," he said, "this time of year."

She nodded and blew out a soft breath. "It's amazing. I'm not the least bit cold, even though it's winter. But I am starving."

"Let's eat then."

Out of the water they pulled on their coats then sat on the mossy bank. The sun was warm and Elly felt

strangely at ease, sitting with Dan wearing only underclothes beneath their jackets, eating thick country
sandwiches of Emmentaler cheese, spicy bratwurst sau-
sage and mustard, nibbling on pickles and washing it
all down with white wine Dan had uncorked for them.
It seemed Cook had thought of everything.

As she finished her sandwich and brushed the
crumbs from her fingers and lap she couldn't help
laughing softly to herself. Dan turned to look at her.
"What?"

"I feel like a high-school kid, sneaking out for a
secret date with a boy."

"Skinny dipped at the beach with the boys, did
you?" He was grinning and she accommodated him by
blushing.

"No. I was boringly shy, I'm afraid. It's taken me
this long to pull a stunt like this."

"But you still drew the line," he said, tipping his
head in the direction of her modest beige bra and panties, peeking out from beneath her coat.

"The remainders of my conservative youth." She
shook her head and smiled but couldn't help letting her
eyes shift to the opening of his jacket and the well-
defined shape within Dan's briefs.

His body in the water that day had been just as
breathtaking as on that first day she'd seen him. Above
the low line of his navy-blue briefs his stomach was
hard and flat. A reddish brown smattering of hair rose
across it and patterned out wider and darker to almost
black across his muscled chest. His shoulders were
beautifully formed—sleek, muscled, shaped by hundreds of strokes along the Haven's beach.

She suddenly wanted him to lie down over her, to
press his muscled torso over her breasts and hips and

let her feel all of him. She wanted this desperately, and with an urgency that felt overpowering. And she wondered where this passion had sprung from when she'd already decided they would never make love.

Yes, she'd been attracted to him from the start, but it had been the kind of attraction she had been able to control. Or maybe it was only that Dan *allowed* her that sense of control. Perhaps the feelings she felt now were a result of sharing their daring escape plan and successfully pulling it off. They were conspirators! Stripping down to swim together and dining on the pebbly beach, laughing at the foolish press they'd so easily tricked…it was all part of a game they'd created. Like naughty children. It was innocent fun.

Or was it? she wondered. Despite their intent to remain just friends, a fragile intimacy had intruded. She was increasingly aware of their provocative state of undress, and of the tempting impulses passing between them.

"I wonder how often we could do it?" Dan mused aloud.

Elly's eyes flew wide open and she stared at him. "Do *what?*" He couldn't be saying what she was thinking.

"Perform our vanishing act."

"Oh, I don't know." She laughed nervously and started to pack sandwich wrappers and leftover pickles back into the string bag. "I suppose they'd catch on after a while."

"We could do this again tomorrow," he suggested. "It's a whole lot better than being cooped up inside the palace, waiting for Jacob and his advisors to come up with their next strategy for dealing with me." He hesitated, then scowled into the distance. "You don't think they'd do anything as drastic as they did in the old days?''

''The old days?''

''Well, in medieval times if you had a rival for the throne, you got rid of him. Classic solution—lock him away. Or poison the poor guy, or just order him killed in his sleep.''

Elly laughed, throwing back her head. ''You do have a wild imagination. Jacob may come off pretty strong sometimes, but I don't think he'd stoop to murdering his own brother, or anyone else for that matter.''

''Hold it right there,'' Dan said, staring intently at her exposed throat.

She froze, thinking he meant to brush a wandering bug from her skin. Instead he leaned across and touched his lips to the sensitive sweep of flesh beneath her chin.

''I've been wanting to do that all day,'' he said in a low voice that sent ripples of heat through her. Then he pulled back and sat tensely, looking away.

She was trembling. She was adrift. Why, she asked herself, was she denying herself this wonderful man's companionship? Because of an irrational fear or a real danger to her life? She wished there was some-one…anyone she could talk to who would understand and help her sort out her life.

A *mother*, she thought sadly. That was who she needed so very badly right now. Her own mother. She would have had the answers. She would have explained why a woman puts her life in a man's hands whenever she enters into intimacy with him. Trust between two people, it was such a fragile thing.

In the distance, an almost indistinguishable sound

shattered her thoughts. She looked up and around. "What was that?"

"I didn't hear anything." Dan leaned toward her as if he was going to kiss her again.

She braced an outstretched palm between them, holding him away so that she could listen. There it was again—a soft growl, as if from a small irritated terrier. She narrowed her eyes and studied the nearby woods, but could see nothing. When the sound came again, it seemed to be coming from the other side of the lake.

"I heard it that time," Dan said. "Could be an animal upset that we've intruded on its home."

Elly nodded. Perhaps. "We should leave," she said. Something told her that whatever had made the strange sound wasn't as harmless as your garden-variety squirrel or groundhog. Anything larger, and she didn't want to meet it.

The next morning Dan awoke to an angry pounding on his door. He squinted at the travel alarm beside his bed and groaned when he saw that it wasn't yet 8:00 a.m. Since there had been no urgency in rising while staying at the castle, he'd grown accustomed to sleeping in. Later that day, with or without Elly, he'd promised himself another excursion to the lake. His mood felt so much improved over the days before.

"Come in," he growled, tugging on the bedclothes to cover his naked hips.

"Get up and get dressed!" a voice ordered smartly.

He scowled as Elly bounded across the chamber, tossing a newspaper onto a chair. She flung open the doors to the armoire on the far side of the room. "And put something decent on. Jacob's in a snit and we're in deep trouble."

"He is? We are?" He sat up in bed trying to make sense of her words. "What's happened now?"

"I found out what that growling noise at the lake was yesterday."

Now he was intrigued. "Yes?"

"You know the sound a thirty-five-millimeter camera makes when it auto-winds?"

The flesh at the back of his neck prickled. "Someone was taking pictures of us at the lake."

"Right." She tossed a pair of khaki pants and a blue oxford shirt onto the bed. "Where is your underwear?"

"I'll take care of my own underwear, thank you." He flung off the covers and she hastily averted her eyes. He would have found the gesture amusing if he wasn't so damn furious. Grabbing the sheet off the bed, he wrapped it around his waist. "How do you know that's what it was?"

"Because of this." She picked up the newspaper she'd brought into the room and pitched it at him. It was a British tabloid. He unfolded it. A full third of the front page displayed a grainy photo of Elly and himself standing in the water. It had been taken at the exact moment he'd given her that companionable peck on the lips. The caption read: The Prince and his Playmate (details, page 3).

"Good grief, how did a photographer get close enough to—"

"Telephoto lens, no doubt," Elly muttered. "He must have either followed us from the castle without our seeing him or he just happened on us then took up a position on the far shore of the lake. You can tell by the angle."

"I see." He handed her the paper with a sinking feeling in his gut. From a drawer he pulled out a clean

T-shirt and briefs, then took his clothes into the bathroom. "So I take it His Highness has seen that paper."

"Yup, and he's furious."

Dan finished buttoning his shirt, tucked in the tails and ran his belt through the loops as he strode back into the bedchamber. "What are we supposed to do about it?"

"I'm not sure, but I expect the first move in such situations is called Facing the Music."

Elly held herself rigidly and let Jacob's outraged words sweep over her. Then she repeated what she'd already told him once before that morning. "No matter how it looks, nothing happened. Besides, it wasn't our fault. We were careful. We just didn't know anyone was there."

But one fact remained, and Elly knew it. By deliberately disobeying Jacob's orders that they remain on the grounds, they had given the press a fresh supply of gossip to weave into all sorts of shocking stories.

"Careful?" Jacob fumed. He thrust two more newspapers across the table at them.

The German journalists were even more inventive than the English. And the French press was having a field day with what they had billed as *le scandale royal*. A photo showed Dan and Elly sitting on the beach, eating their lunch. Beneath the photo, which had obviously been altered, was an easily translatable French subtitle: Unidentified Lover of the New Prince Bares It All. The photo had been touched up, removing the bra Elly had never taken off and supplying her with another woman's breasts.

Dan watched Elly go stone-white as she stared in horror at the photo. Tears trembled at the corners of her eyes. He felt awful for her. This was so much worse for her than for him. "This is a blatant invasion of privacy!" he growled. "Can't anything be done?"

"You took it upon yourselves to disrobe in a public place." Jacob glared at him accusingly. "If the photographer had broken into the castle that would be another thing."

"But I told you, we weren't *doing* anything," Elly said weakly, looking at Allison who had just entered the room. "We just went for a swim, decently covered, then ate lunch on the beach."

Allison shook her head in sympathy. But before she could speak her husband jumped in. "The point is, it doesn't appear to the observer that all was innocent. Even if the photographer altered the print, the fact remains...the two of your were frolicking in a secluded lake with next to nothing on!"

"Oh, don't be a prude, dear," Allison said with a sigh, shocking Elly with her casual tone. "You remember what being in love was like." She gave her husband a secretive look. Elly suspected the royal couple was still very much in love from the responding glimmer of a smile from Jacob. "Besides, you can't honestly expect everyone to remain shut up in the palace indefinitely. That's no solution."

"With a little more time, everything would have settled down," Jacob grumbled.

"With a little more time, the paparazzi would have dug up more stories about your father's playboy years," Dan snapped. "I don't see what good is being done by our being here at all."

The two men glared at each other.

The gulf between the two brothers was clearly widening. Elly wished there was something she could do to help them work together, but she feared it was already too late for that.

Six

Elly hid her deepest and most personal rage and humiliation from Dan. She had decided before she told him about the newspaper photos that her reaction was crucial to his. If she let him know how hurt she'd been, that would only make him all the angrier. And right now the only thing that would save them all was clear thinking.

But she couldn't totally ignore her own fears: her fear that her father's business, and therefore he himself, would be irreparably damaged by the new scandal she and Dan had unwittingly instigated, and then there was her fear for her own future. She no longer believed she could remain alone all of her life. Yet the thought of being with other men, men who didn't want a family, felt far less appealing than spending long, loving days with Dan, whose warmth, generosity and passion came so naturally to him. She longed to play a role in his life, but couldn't begin to figure out how. Then there was the worry, eating away at her, that by bringing Dan to Elbia she hadn't brought two brothers together, she had started a war. And she now had escalated that war by sneaking off with Dan against his brother's orders.

The day after word of their woodland tryst broke, the royal press secretary delivered copies of newspapers from a dozen countries, including the U.S., to the dining room. Although most were the sleazy, gossip rags that harassed movie stars and politicians, a few respected publications showed the same embarrassing photographs on inside pages. The articles were short, sketchy and less accusatory. Still, she felt nauseated seeing herself and Dan in such intimate poses, for all the world to view. And it wasn't as if they'd done anything wrong! she kept reminding herself. She'd been discreet, revealing no more than a modest bathing suit would, and they'd shared no more than a kiss.

Elly sighed and stopped walking on her way back from the empty dining room where she'd had just juice and a bagel for a late breakfast. She looked out a window into the garden. Madge and Frank were sitting on a stone bench in a sunny spot, looking cozy in their warm jackets. Madge took a photograph from her coat pocket and showed it to him. He smiled and nodded, and seemed to be commenting on it. She assumed it was a picture of Dan as a child. One proud parent sharing memories with another. That was nice. At least two people in this castle were getting along, she thought ruefully.

The sound of voices came to Elly from the end of the long hallway hung with rich tapestries. Elly looked up to see Allison heading her way, little Prince Cray holding her hand, a nurse carrying baby Kristina. Elly smiled at the little group. What a joy to have two little ones as beautiful and cheerful as these two. What she wouldn't give to be brave enough to...

She cut off the thought...the wish...the dream that could never be.

Elly put on a smile for the children. "Well, hello! How are you two doing today?"

"Great!" Cray chirped. "I talked on the terror-phone."

Elly laughed. "You mean, the *telephone*."

"Actually, he can be a bit of a terror on the phone," Allison said with a sigh. "When it rings in the nursery, he races us for it and wants to do all the talking him-self." She patted her son affectionately on the head. "We're heading back to the nursery. Would you like to come along?"

Elly involuntarily tightened inside. But she couldn't resist. "I'd like that. May I?" she asked, offering to take the baby.

Kristina held out her pudgy little arms and gurgled at her. The nurse handed her over.

"She's so beautiful." Elly stroked the tiny, soft head and its blond curls.

"We think so," Allison murmured, love shining in her eyes. She tousled her son's hair, so as not to leave him out, and he grinned mischievously up at her. Then Allison turned to Elly with a different expression en-tirely. "I'm sorry you're having such a difficult time with the press. It isn't fair that your privacy should be invaded this way. Dan seems like a nice man too. It can't be easy for him."

"It's not," Elly said solemnly. "He must feel so very helpless, and he's a man used to action. You know, seeing a problem then doing something to resolve it. This time his hands are tied."

"Dealing with the public through a voracious press has been the hardest thing for me to adjust to," Allison admitted. "I've only been in Elbia and married to Jacob for less than two years, you see. Before then, the only contact I had with a newspaper was writing announcements for children's story hours at the library in the community events column."

Elly didn't want to say that she was aware the birth of their son had preceded the couple's marriage, but the lovely American's marriage to the bachelor prince of Elbia had been a lead story in newspapers and magazines everywhere. Their wedding had been the focus of TV and radio talk shows, and the ceremony itself had been telecast by satellite all over the world. Now that she had met Allison in person, she wondered how this woman, no older than herself, had survived those unbelievably stressful days.

But now Allison seemed both content with her surroundings and comfortable with her role as Jacob's queen. Elly noticed that the staff, though respectful of her, never seemed nervous around or fearful of their mistress. Allison never ordered them about but quietly asked for their help when she needed it and always thanked them afterwards. There was no question that their queen was beloved by her subjects.

"How do you live with the prying and lack of privacy, day in and day out?" Elly asked. "I think I'd go mad."

"It's not often this bad," Allison admitted as they continued walking. "Usually, we're very open with the journalists, and they respect the times we ask to be left alone. It's only when we travel that things sometimes get a little rough.'' She reached out to touch her daughter's cheek in a protective gesture.

''How much longer will my swimming escapade prolong their interest?''

Allison smiled at her. ''Good grief, it's not as if you were totally nude, skinny dipping with the entire football squad!'' She laughed merrily, making light of the situation, and Elly instantly felt better. ''Oh, who can say. A couple of weeks? Maybe longer, it depends. Sad to say, if there were a terrible disaster somewhere in the world or a popular celebrity died, most of them would rush off to cover the new story and forget all about you.''

''I don't know if anyone can stand another two weeks shut up here. It's so unfair to the rest of you, suffering for my mistake.''

Allison shrugged. ''We'll make do. Have you seen Dan today? How is he taking things now? Any calmer?''

''I haven't dared search him out.'' Elly shook her head. ''Last I saw him, he was brooding and looking unapproachable.''

''Typical male.''

Elly grinned. ''A lot like his brother, is he?''

''Mirror image. It's spooky when I watch them together. If they could only accept each other and work together.''

''That's just what I've been thinking,'' Elly admitted. ''But it may be hopeless.''

''Give them time,'' Allison advised. ''They have a lot to work out.''

Elly knew that was true. Just as she and Dan had a lot to resolve, which was something she'd been trying desperately to ignore. Emotions left unspoken, feelings too fragile to put into words, hopes that might come crashing down and shatter at the mere whisper of the truth.

She tucked her thoughts away within her heart, not yet ready to admit to them. After all, there was a good chance Dan would never speak to her again after this latest incident.

Two days earlier, Dan had been so angry he didn't dare stay in the same room with anyone. He checked on Madge in her room and apologized for embarrassing her.

She had seemed more amused than upset by the photos, as if relieved that the spotlight had shifted away from her indiscretions and had now turned to the younger generation's.

"It won't happen again," he assured her.

She didn't comment on that. "Elizabeth seems a very nice girl," she said. "I didn't like her very much at first, but I suppose she was just doing her job."

He blinked at his mother. Was this her way of saying she *approved* of Elly? He left without asking for clarification. Too much was already on his mind. Too many decisions had to be made, and quickly.

On the third day, he woke up with a clear head and a few ideas. He dressed and, before he'd had breakfast, found his way to the press secretary's office and asked for the morning's newspapers. They were just as he suspected they'd be. Each still carried a risqué photo of him and Elly, some from slightly different angles, as if the photographer had moved along the bank of the lake, snapping away. The captions were more outrageous than ever and featured stories to match. He asked to borrow the papers for a short while and marched off with them wedged under one arm.

It was only eight o'clock, but he knocked firmly on Elly's door and when he heard a sleepy, "Come in," he let himself in.

"Oh," she said, "I was hoping it was one of Allison's marvelous clairvoyant servants with coffee."

"Coffee can wait," he said briskly and tossed the stack of papers down on her bed.

She gazed at them dejectedly, turning a shade paler. "I don't think I can stomach any more of this."

"Look at them," he ordered.

She scowled. "This is cruel and unusual punishment, particularly this early in the morning. Besides, you're the one who suggested we go for a swim. In fact, if it wasn't for me, we'd have both been caught on film for posterity with—"

"With our posteriors showing, I know. But look at the damn papers."

She groaned. "You are an impossible man."

"I know." He grinned at her. "Now pay attention, I'm going to quiz you in a minute."

Elly sat up in bed and pulled the stack of newsprint into her lap. Today the photos seemed a little smaller, taking up space on inside rather than front pages. Apparently, shots of less clarity had been saved to be run later. Anyone looking at the pictures would assume from the attitudes and nearness of the man and woman in the photo that they were lovers. Even at a distance, the way she and Dan were looking at each other revealed an intimate connection and a longing that, for all the viewer knew, might have been satisfied moments after the picture had been shot.

"What do you see?" Dan asked her.

"Good grief, need you ask?"

"What do you see?" he repeated.

"Two lovers," she groaned.

"Maybe, but look at the caption."

She grimaced but read it aloud. "The Secret Prince and His Mysterious Lover."

"And the story?"

"Do I have to?" Elly wailed.

"Read the first three paragraphs of this one." He pushed a New York daily at her.

She read to herself then looked up at him. "It's total fantasy. Ludicrous. They have no idea what they're talking about. This part about your challenging Jacob for the throne is complete—"

"Rubbish, I know." He sat on the bed beside her. "And so are the stories in the Chicago *Journal* and the LA *News* and the London *Express*. In every single paper, reporters are trying to weave stories from rumors. They have no facts upon which to base their speculations."

"Good!" She shoved the noxious tabloids off her lap.

"No," he said slowly, "not good. Not yet." He gave her a devilish grin.

She frowned at him. "You're scaring me. The last scheme that warped mind of yours cooked up got us into worse trouble!"

He ignored her concern. "I was awake most of the night thinking about this mess. And it occurred to me that we're tackling the problem all wrong. Hiding out only makes my presence more intriguing. And covering up the facts of my mother's liaison with Karl only makes the story seem more lurid and mysterious than it really is. And people love mysteries."

"Almost as much as they love gossip about the rich," Elly said.

"Right. So it's my theory that Jacob should hold a press conference. Go public with everything we know, as soon as possible. Let them take pictures of all of us and ask whatever questions they feel like asking. Get it all out into the air."

"And what about us? What about those pictures of you and me in compromising non-attire?"

"The truth, again."

Elly looked doubtful. And in a way he was lying to her on this one count, because he wasn't going to tell the world that what they saw in those photos was exactly what he had been feeling. He had wanted to make passionate love to Elly. He had wanted to strip off that dripping bra and tear away her nearly useless panties and see all of her and have all of her. The pictures hadn't lied about what was in his heart, although they had misrepresented what they'd eventually not done.

"The truth is," he continued, "we were feeling stir crazy after being trapped inside the castle for days and decided to break out and go for a walk. The swimming was on a whim, and the kiss was between friends and never went any further than that. They can believe it or not. The key is, after things ease up and Jacob and I work out our relationship, which could be just a matter of a few days, I'll be returning to Maryland and you'll be going your own way. Then no one will have anything to whisper about."

Elly looked at him, wide-eyed, as if turning his words over in her mind. "That's true," she murmured, tossing back the bedclothes and standing up beside the bed. "It will be over." She sounded more than a little sad at the thought, but he couldn't be sure that he wasn't reading his own feelings into her words.

"So what do you say we take my plan to Jacob?" he asked.

She shook her head and paced away from him. "He flew to Vienna yesterday...some sort of economic meeting with heads of state from a handful of other European countries. But I think he's supposed to be back tomorrow afternoon."

"Good, we'll hold down the fort until then and fine-tune my plan."

He caught her looking at him, and there was a tenderness in her expression that took him by surprise. "What are you thinking?" he asked softly.

She reached out slowly, as if some inner spirit had possessed her and she was no longer in control of her actions. Her fingertips brushed the short hairs in front of his ear. "You'll make a wonderful father."

He laughed, not understanding. "Huh?"

"You never stay angry, and you work out problems. Your children will feel secure, knowing you will be fair and not blame them for their mistakes. And they'll understand that you will always be there for them, to help them solve their problems. Pretty important dad stuff."

His eyes latched onto hers. A woman who understood a man's need to be gentle, lenient, fair and protective of his children was rare indeed. But there was also his need to know her, completely. He wanted to touch her mind, understand the demons that stood in the way of her trusting him, and find a way to work around them. He ached to bring her peace.

Then somehow, all those charitable feelings took a sudden, unexpected twist, and he found himself overcome by a primitive male urge to seize her and make love to her despite her earlier rejections. He hated himself for feeling that way, for even considering taking her against her will. But the primal hunger was there beneath the civilized man, as it was in every male. The heat in his loins grew and a pounding in his head blocked out rational thought. The muscles in his arms ached, and even as he looked down at her he could feel what it would be like to seize her and possess her as he had in a thousand dreams.

The only thing that separates us from animals is our ability to choose not to act, he reminded himself, fiercely holding back.

"What's wrong?" she asked, stepping closer to him and studying his expression with concern as her fingertips grazed his cheek. Her nightgown clung to her slim body, revealing too much, or not enough...he couldn't decide.

Had he spoken out loud? "Nothing," he said, turning away from her. Then something made him change his mind. "Damn it, Elly, it *wasn't* nothing."

He gripped her shoulders, and her still-raised hand dropped from his cheek to his chest as her mouth opened in surprise. "I've wanted you since the day we met. I've let you know how deeply you move me, how special I think you are. But you hold me at arm's length then turn me away. If you feel nothing for me, just say so. I won't bother you again."

She stared up at him, her lower lip trembling. "Dan, please. You know it's not like that."

"How is it then?" he demanded, fighting the impulse to throw her down on the bed. "You know I won't let you get pregnant if that's not what you want. Don't you trust me?"

"I do..." She began to sob as her eyes filled with tears. "Of course I trust you. I just. I *can't*...don't you see?" She couldn't get the words out for her gulping sobs.

"No, I don't see, obviously. Here is a man who wants the woman standing before him, and a woman who is so in need of a good man in her life she quivers when he comes too close. *We want the same thing, Elly!*"

"No! No, we don't!" She shook her head violently, trying to step away. But he held her firmly by the arms, not allowing her to retreat. "We've gone over this before. It's not just about now, this minute, this hour in our lives...it's about the future. I know what my limits are, and I've learned to accept them. I'll never be able to give you what you want, a child. Perhaps more than one. Let's not fool ourselves." She stared up at him, her eyes shimmering pools. "Please. If I can be strong enough to walk away from you, feeling as close to you as I do right now, you can certainly be strong enough to *let* me walk away."

With a lump in his throat he released her, but only to let her move two steps away from him before grabbing her hand and tugging her back to face him. He stepped up to within inches of her. "I'm not that strong."

She shook her head, tears clinging to her lashes. "Oh, Dan."

He cradled her against his chest. "Let's not try to map out our entire lives in one night. Life never turns out as we expect anyway, does it?"

She moved her head again, more softly, less frantically, her lips brushing the fabric of his shirt. "No, it doesn't."

"So, Miss Anderson, tell me this..." He took a deep breath, risking all. "For the next few hours, do you think we could give each other what we most desire just *at this moment* and not think about the past or about some time years down the line?"

She didn't answer immediately, and a white-hot stab of fear shot through him. Then her whisper soothed him. "I'd like to try."

His heart soared and, to his consternation, his body responded with energy. If she felt his hardness between them, she gave no indication, unless the slightly amused tilt of her smile was for that reason.

Dan slowly lowered his head and kissed her deeply, holding back none of his passion. Before, he'd never been sure that she felt as much for him as he felt for her. But now the commitment seemed equal. They were partners in an act of love, neither one aggressor or victim, seducer or seduced. They stood on even ground and that pleased him. Their pact made it possible for him to forget, for the time being, the family he might have to wait longer for or never have. And their agreement apparently made it possible for her to make love with him without guilt for depriving him of his dream or threatening her life.

They would keep each other safe and they would pleasure each other, and to hell with anything else.

Her lips opened willingly to his. As he moved his hands over her body he gave silent thanks for having picked up his wallet when he'd left his room an hour earlier. For there was the key to Elly, the condom he would willingly wear to reassure her that she was safe with him.

In fact there was more than one in there. Who knew what had possessed him to jam two long strips into the thin leather tri-fold, but he'd been in a rush while packing and perhaps he'd had a momentary crazed vision of dark-eyed foreign women throwing themselves at him as he stepped off the plane in Paris, so there they were. He was just glad he had ample protection because he had a feeling they might need every one of them.

He pulled three foil packets from his wallet and placed them in clear view on the night table. Elly blushed as her eyes rested on them.

"You're beautiful when you're embarrassed," he whispered. "Let's see if we can embarrass you some more."

She looked up at him with a slightly dazed expression as he kissed her again and slipped the straps of her nightgown off her shoulders and down her arms. The garment slid from her body to the floor in a puddle of pale silk. She wore nothing beneath it and, although he'd known that would be so, the sight of her completely nude before him ripped the breath from his lungs. In the words of his city kids, she was awesome.

He sensed she had averted her eyes, and he lifted his gaze to her face and gently nudged her chin with his knuckles to make her look at him. "Don't be ashamed of what we're doing."

"I'm not...I'm—" Her eyes blazed and her cheeks flushed a lovely dark color. "I feel freed, I feel wonderful." She hesitated, looking suddenly shy again. "Do you suppose we could even up the odds a little?" Her eyes swept slowly down his shirt front to his pants.

He laughed, delighted with her. "Yes, ma'am." He couldn't remember ever getting undressed quite as fast as he did that day. Within seconds he'd flung belt, pants, shirt, underclothes, shoes and socks into a heap.

He remembered thinking that first day they'd met on the beach that he'd have loved to have been swimming naked, just to see her expression. Now he received his reward for waiting. Her eyes were wide, glassy, and she kept passing the tip of her tongue over her lips as if they were parched by desert heat. Her hands clasped in front of her, and she tipped her head to one side, observing him critically, as if he were sculpture in a museum.

"So what's the verdict?" He stepped toward her.

"Not bad. Not bad at all." A smile teased the corners of her lips.

"That's all I get? A not bad?" he growled then grabbed her.

They fell onto the bed and Elly could no longer keep up her smug act. Her heart was pounding in her breast. Every nerve in her body tingled with anticipation. For the first time in her life, she was with a man who was about to make love to her, and the dark side of life seemed miles away. She thought of nothing but opening her body to Dan.

She kept her eyes open when he kissed her. She didn't want to miss a thing, and the sight of Dan was glorious, for he was sleek and muscled, and every angle and curve of his body was pure masculine poetry. When he lifted one arm to curl it around her and bring her closer to his chest, the muscles in his shoulder and biceps bunched just as they had when he stroked through the ocean. When he moved her into his chest, she lifted a finger to trace the conformation that might have been carved by a master sculptor. She marveled at each pale blue vein, each tiny mole, each sinew that swelled across his wide chest.

"You are amazing," she whispered. But when she

looked up, the cocky grin she imagined she'd find on his lips wasn't there. They were tightly pressed together as if he was concentrating on a matter of grave importance. And his eyes blazed. His gaze never seemed to move from her face, but she knew he was studying her entire body. The intensity made her shiver.

"Don't be afraid," he said.

"I'm not. I'm just waiting."

"Not for long." Now he did smile, but it was as much a warning as a promise of pleasure. It said, *Hold on tight, woman, here we go.*

He moved over her, supporting himself on one forearm while he caressed the soft swell of her hip. The muscles in her limbs grew rigid but in a most pleasant way. He smoothed his fingertips down the outside of her thigh then up the inside, toward the pulsing lips of her womanhood. Elly lifted herself to meet them, and he found her and pressed softly inward until she let out a little gasp of delight. His touch grew firmer, centering around her most sensitive area, circling, stroking, raising golden tongues of fire within her. Her head spun. Her limbs ached as she locked them against his body, and his fingers continued to work their magic.

She felt as if something snapped within her, something that was supposed to break—a bond, a chain tying her to the past. At a sudden rush of heat, she opened her mouth on a scream of ecstasy, but Dan cut it off with a plunging kiss. Delicious sensations burst through her with the brilliance of fireworks—dazzling, surprising her with their intensity. And all this from the mere touch of his hand.

Elly was aware of Dan shifting on the bed beside her, heard the sound of tearing foil and almost immediately he returned to her. She didn't have to look to know he had kept his promise. Nevertheless, he took her hand and gently guided it down along his body and folded her fingers around his sheathed shaft to reassure her.

"I know," she whispered. "I know."

He was over her now, sweeping her hair away from her face with both hands as he held his upper body over her on his elbows. Their hips pressed together. She felt the heaviness of his masculinity, the warm furriness of him against the tops of her thighs. Slowly she lifted her knees, parted herself and wrapped her legs around his hips to welcome him.

He only had to raise his own hips and move upward an inch to find her. Then with no effort at all, he entered her, filling her, it seemed, completely. The world hummed around her and her eyes closed on the blissful sensation of completion. As a woman, as a lover, as the giver of tenderness and passion that she had always longed to be.

But that blissful moment of peace lasted only seconds, for then Dan was moving within her, raising her with him to undreamed-of heights, cupping his palms beneath her bottom and lifting her hips to meet his thrusts as he delved deeper and deeper within her until she was sure there could be no more room for him. And Elly tightened around him, bursting with honeyed answer to his perfectly timed strokes, and she turned her face into the wiry fur of his chest and let out a smothered whimper of ecstasy that seemed to roll on forever.

At last Dan arched his body above hers, his eyes tightly shut, his face contorted in agonizing pleasure, as he pressed hard into her with a low groan of male satisfaction. He fell in exhaustion upon her, and she wrapped herself around him, holding him within her for as long as the silvery forever of one morning allowed.

Seven

Conversation around the breakfast table the following morning seemed distant and insignificant to Elly. Another day had passed but an invisible, golden thread still stretched between herself and Dan—and though no one in the dining room could see it, she knew it was there. A unique connection held her to the beautiful man who sat across the table from her.

Dan ate quickly, barely looking at her during the meal except for a single meaningful glance when no one else was looking. Then he excused himself and left the room. Shortly afterward, Elly bid her father, Madge, and Allison good bye for the rest of the day, saying she had work to finish and would spend the day at it, probably skipping lunch. Her father gave her a puzzled look but said nothing.

Elly was back in her room for only half an hour before Dan appeared, as she somehow knew he would.

The previous day, after they had parted, had been busy for both, and there had been no time when they could be alone.

Dan followed his own best advice: he focused on the moment. These precious few hours when Elly was his. If he just concentrated on the way she made him feel, he could forget about the mad twist of fate life had dealt him. Forget about the press and the public hysteria, which might do all sorts of damage to the Haven. Forget about how humiliating all of this was for his mother. Forget that each minute he held Elly might be their last together and certainly brought them closer to the time they must part.

He made love to her immediately on joining her in her room, then two more times during the long, lazy hours of the day in between conversations that covered everything from their childhoods to hopes for their careers, favorite colors, and most-beloved music, foods, and books. Then, at last, Elly looked up at him with smiling, misty eyes and said the abhorrent words, "We have to go down for dinner."

"Can't we ring for room service?" he begged.

"This isn't a hotel. Besides, I think someone might suspect something. Particularly after our much-publicized romp in the lake."

"Oh that." He groaned then pulled her close and whispered softly into her ear. "When we're together, all the bad stuff goes away. Doesn't it?"

"Yes. All of it," she murmured with a touch of amazement in her sweet voice.

His heart melted at the sincerity in her voice, for he knew the "bad stuff" for her had been very black indeed, the fear that had been her mother's unintended legacy to her. It seemed a miracle that she'd been able to leave those fears behind, at last, to be with him and him alone. No one else had been able to give her that. He felt empowered, as if he'd been singled out to perform this special task in her life.

"Come on," she said, leaving the bed to pull him to his feet. "Put some clothes on. With any luck, Jacob will have returned and you can explain your master plan to him."

Dan frowned. "Do you think he'll even listen? He hasn't exactly been a loving and compassionate brother."

She gave him a semi-severe look. "I haven't seen you falling over backward to please him either. There's definitely a family gene that leans toward stubbornness."

"You think so?"

"I know so. Now, dress!"

Dan took his place at the heavy wooden trestle table across from Allison with her two children on either side of her. Jacob had indeed returned and was at the head of the table, with his family to his right. Dan sat to his left, then came Elly, then Madge, with Frank Anderson sitting across from her.

Although seated beside Dan, Elly felt as if he was miles from her after the intimacy of the day and the night before. She cast him a longing look but snapped her eyes down to her plate when she felt her father's curious gaze on her.

Allison made small talk, asking how Jacob's trip had gone and he responded with vague observations. He looked distracted, and Elly saw him glance more than once at Dan, as if he wanted to say something but couldn't find the right words. Dan shot his brother worried looks, as if he too was searching for the right words. Tension slowly filled the room, like hot water being poured from a steaming pitcher.

Meanwhile a magnificent meal was being served. Each course was presented by Cook's competent kitchen staff. Elly was beginning to recognize them and learn their names. Rachel was very young, born in Elbia. She wore her hair in braids, looped up beneath a white cap. Friedrich was a tall, gaunt-looking man with gray hair and a stern demeanor that softened whenever his eyes came to rest on the little prince and princess. He had come from Vienna over thirty years ago to serve the von Austerand family. Maria was a dark, middle-aged Italian woman, chief assistant to Cook, who prepared many of the meals herself but insisted on overseeing the service to the family.

The other dining-room attendants rotated, according to the meal, but usually Elly recognized them. She studied a new man. He moved carefully about the room, ladling soup from a gilded porcelain tureen. Unlike the regulars, when he stood between two diners he served to the guest on his right then to the one on his left, rather than moving around the table to always serve toward the right as, she'd noticed, was convention. She glanced at Maria to see if she'd caught the minor slip in protocol, but she was turning back toward the kitchen.

It seemed an unimportant detail to Elly, yet something about the man felt not quite right to her. She turned toward Dan and found his gaze steadily on her. Frowning, she slid her eyes in the direction of the server, then gave Dan a questioning quirk of one eyebrow.

He followed her line of sight, watched the man for a moment, then shrugged.

He was right, it was probably nothing, she told herself. A hurried replacement by an inexperienced waiter. She turned her attention back to the conversation at the table.

Cray was babbling happily about his day's activities, everything from his adventures with learning to talk on the telephone to telling his father, the king, about his finger-painting exploits. "It was gooey and slippery, and all over the paper and table and floor and me!" he cried with delight. "Green and red and blue *everywhere!*" He waved his hands in the air to demonstrate the degree of delightful messiness he'd created. Everyone one at the table congratulated Cray on his artistic efforts.

As his mother was inviting all guests to come to the nursery for a viewing of his first exhibition, a motion just barely caught the corner of Elly's eye. She turned her head to follow it.

The new server stood beside the tall mahogany buffet along one side of the room, across from the little prince and princess. As Elly watched, he turned as though to shield something in his hand from view, and she heard a soft click.

Her breath caught in her throat. *What was he doing? What was he holding that he didn't want anyone to see?*

She reached out to touch Dan on the shoulder, but apparently he'd also been watching the man. Dan shot to his feet, knocking his chair backward with a crash to the floor. To the other guests' amazement, he launched himself across the room and, before the server could react, Dan had tackled the man and pinned him to the floor.

"Call your security!" he bellowed at Jacob.

The king didn't need to say a word. Three burly guards appeared within seconds in the dining room. Elly suspected cameras hidden somewhere in the room had caught the struggle.

There was pandemonium as Jacob jumped to his feet, Cray shouted out questions, Kristina started to cry and Frank Anderson glared in confusion at Dan as if he'd committed an act of terrorism. Elly could only stand by until things sorted themselves out.

Two of the guards relieved Dan of his prisoner while a third smoothly placed his body between the intruder and the royal family. Jacob, she'd noticed, had instinctively moved in front of Allison and the children, as if to shield them.

One of the guards removed a small, black object from inside the folds of the intruder's white smock.

"Is that a gun?" Madge gasped.

The guard held a miniature camera up for Jacob to see.

"I'm a respected member of the press!" the man shouted in English. An American, Elly thought with a sinking feeling in her stomach. This isn't good. "We have freedom of speech in my country—and that's personal property!"

Dan stood close by, glaring at the man. "You don't have the right to break into a man's home or terrorize his family, you idiot!"

But the guards were already dragging the man through a door and, in another minute, a shocked silence hung over those remaining in the dining room.

"Oh my," Madge breathed, pressing a hand to her heart.

"Are you all right?" Elly asked.

"Yes, I'm fine. It's the little ones I'm worried about." She looked at Cray and Kristina, the prince clinging to his mother's skirt, the baby in her arms.

"It's all right now," Allison said to her children comfortingly. "The stranger is gone now. I think we need some quiet time." She looked meaningfully at Jacob. He nodded. "Let's go have a story in your nursery. We'll ask Cook very nicely to bring our dessert to us there, for a special treat." The third guard automatically accompanied the queen and her children out of the dining room.

"I think I'll go to my room too," Madge murmured, looking shaken despite her denial. "I have a headache."

"That was quite a shock," Elly said. "You should rest for a while. Do you feel steady enough on your feet?"

"I'll manage," she said, but her smile seemed wobbly.

"I'll walk her back to her room," Frank said quickly, giving Dan a reassuring look.

Elly, Dan and Jacob were the only ones left in the room along with the disarray of a half-finished meal. Dan righted his chair. No one spoke for a long while, then it was Jacob who finally sat down heavily at the head of the table and looked up at the two Americans.

"That shouldn't have happened." He sighed. "Thank you."

"For what?" Dan asked simply. "It was just another reporter with a camera."

"It might have been something else." Jacob gave

his brother a long, grim look. "If that had been a gun, the guards would have spotted it and come in, but in the few extra seconds he could have gotten off a shot."

"Elly saw him first but I was closest to him. No big deal."

"But you put your life in jeopardy for my family," Jacob insisted. "For all you knew he could have shot or stabbed you to get to me, or to my wife and babies. You didn't hesitate. I will never forget this. Never." He stared hard at Dan with an electric intensity that crackled around them.

Elly could feel the testosterone level in the room rise. This was male bonding at its best. She would have smiled if the circumstances had been different. "What will happen to the man?" she asked.

Jacob shrugged. "Not much. We'll hold him for a few days, put the fear of God in him. His newspaper will protest. The U.S. Embassy will appeal to us. Then we'll allow your government officials to escort him out of the country." He gave her a funny look. "Did you expect me to lock him away in the dungeon for eternity?"

She laughed. "Something like that, I suppose. Your Highness—" she hesitated "—this has to stop."

"Yes," he agreed. He looked at Dan. "I respect your reasons for not wanting to release your claim to my father's name...*our* father's name. And I understand why you won't accept a financial settlement. In your shoes, I would feel much the same way." Maria stepped gingerly into the room, but Jacob waved her off. "That leaves us in an awkward situation, though. I don't know what to do now."

"I have an idea," Dan said, slowly lowering himself

into the chair nearest Jacob's. "I thought of it yesterday and wanted to talk to you then, but you weren't here."

Jacob nodded. "Go on."

Elly crossed her fingers for Dan. Jacob was listening with guarded interest, but there was no guarantee he'd agree to Dan's strategy.

"Maybe we've been going at this all wrong," Dan started. "By trying to hide the truth and giving the press no facts at all, we've only made them more intrigued with the possibilities. They smell scandal and won't let up until the story seems no longer interesting to them. As long as we remain silent, they'll invent new and provocative stories to suit their readers' curiosity."

"Let me understand this…you think we should find a way to *bore* them?" Jacob gave a weary smile. "Difficult to do, brother, for people like us. We announce a vacation to Australia, and it becomes a mission of political importance. When Allison purchased a new bed for Cray, half the mothers in Europe bought the same brand for their toddlers."

"Not bore them…*defuse* them. Call a press conference, make it open to anyone. We'll issue a joint statement saying that you and I are in complete accord. I'm thrilled to have found my father's family, and you're overjoyed to have located your long-lost brother."

Jacob rolled his eyes. "Laying it on a little thick, aren't we?"

Dan shrugged. "We have to put a positive spin on this. I'll accept the monetary settlement, but it will be on behalf of my mother, for her future care, and for my City Kids program. That portion will be used to build and support a year-round camp for kids at risk who need to be pulled off the street and given a safe place to be for a while.''

Jacob looked interested. ''And what about the throne? You are older than I by several months. By rights, even though my father and your mother weren't married, you are the first heir.''

Dan shook his head. ''I wouldn't want your job for anything, bro'.''

Elly smiled at the slang, which also brought a wry twitch to Jacob's lips.

''There are some definite advantages,'' Jacob said, lifting a hand to indicate the grandeur of this single room among the hundreds of richly appointed rooms in the castle.

''This wouldn't make me happy,'' Dan said. He shot a look at Elly, and she blushed. ''Other things are much more important to me. I'll sign a release relinquishing all rights to my royal status. If the Duke of Windsor could do it, so can I.''

Jacob's eyes remained steadily on Dan, as if reassessing him. ''And there is nothing else you ask?''

''Not a blamed thing.''

Elly felt so proud of Dan. She stepped to his side and touched him on the arm to tell him so.

''It's a good plan, but I think we can improve on it,'' Jacob mused, leaning back into his chair and spearing a piece of asparagus with his fork. ''We will have the press conference and announce everything just as you have suggested. But—'' he pointed the fork tines at Dan for emphasis ''—the announcement will be made at a grand ball, in your and your mother's honor.''

Dan looked worried. ''I don't think that's necess—''

''Humor me,'' Jacob said, straightening in his chair.

"I don't often get a chance to outwit our aggressive brothers in the paparazzi. If we are to convince them that I am welcoming the cherished lost branch of my family, then we must make a grand show of it. As you've said...a positive spin to beat all positive spins."

Elly grinned. "I think it will work, Dan. Really."

Jacob looked as if he was enjoying the game. "Instead of a rivalry, they will witness brothers helping each other and celebrating their finding each other. Then, to further distract the press, we will invite so many celebrities they won't know who to focus on. The truth about my father's long-ago affair and Daniel Eastwood's birth will seem far less interesting to them."

Dan looked thoughtful. Then he turned to Elly with a questioning look.

"Go for it," she said. But she couldn't help adding wickedly, "Although I can't imagine shooting pictures of you if Tom Cruise were in the room."

"Thanks," Dan said dryly. He turned back to his brother. "Make a note not to invite Mr. Cruise."

As soon as the announcement of the ball was made, Allison requested the services of her favorite seamstress.

"It must be wonderful to have someone who can make anything you want to wear," Elly commented wistfully as she sat in the nursery playing with Kristina the day the dressmaker arrived.

"It's actually a very practical and cost-effective arrangement," Allison said. She was chasing Cray around the room with a hair brush in hand. He was at the stage where he didn't like to be fussed over, and hair brushing was the worst sort of torture as far as he was concerned. "I know many women of the aristocracy who wouldn't wear anything less than couturier. Helena knows my taste exactly and will make me a one-of-a-kind gown or traveling suit for a fraction of the cost of a Parisian design.''

Elly laughed. ''You watch your clothing budget that closely? Why, with all the money floating around this place?''

Allison shrugged. ''Habit, I suppose. For a long time I had to pinch pennies just to support myself and Cray on a librarian's income. That was before his father came back into our lives. But I also think it's obscene to spend a fortune on clothing when the money could go toward helping people who really need it.''

Elly looked with admiration at the young American who had so recently become queen of the little country. She had grace, goodness and beauty. ''I think that's wonderful,'' she murmured. ''So what is Helena making for you this time?''

''Nothing, actually,'' Allison replied, winking at Helena as the woman unpacked her measuring tapes, notepad and swatches of fabric. ''She's come to fit you.''

''Me?''

''I doubt you came prepared with formal wear, given your hasty escape from the States.''

''That's true, but—''

''And with the paparazzi still guarding the castle gates, it's impractical for you to consider going into town to shop for a dress. Of course, if you really insist, we could airlift you in the helicopter to Vienna, but that's just as expensive as Paris these days.''

''Oh, no!'' Elly protested. ''I don't want to put you to any trouble. Frankly, I hadn't even thought of a dress. I'm just glad that Jacob and Dan seem to be working together now instead of fighting.''

"I am too," Allison admitted, finally tackling Cray and bringing him kicking and squirming into her lap.

After a while, Gretchen, the children's nurse, relieved the two women of the little ones so that they could concentrate on a gown for Elly. She chose a pale green silk to compliment her red hair, with cream-colored lace trim. After admiring Allison's closet-full of gowns with full, bouffant skirts, she worked out a very different, fitted design with Helena that started in a strapless bodice, clung to her waist and hips, then tapered to the floor in the back. In the front, the skirt was cut nearly as high as her knees to reveal her shapely legs. It was a sophisticated, sensual style that made her feel as elegant as any princess.

In a separate wing of the castle, Jacob met with Dan to discuss the details of their statement to the press. Dan listened to the wording Jacob's secretary had drafted and read aloud to them, his fingers peaked before his lips in concentration. Three other advisors, a woman and two men, also listened in, taking notes, looking terribly serious. The tension in the room was thick, and no one spoke until the reading was finished.

Then, in the silence, everyone looked at Jacob for a reaction. "I have no objection to anything there," he said slowly. "I believe we've covered it all—the surrender of claim on the throne, the compensation...which I hope is sufficient?" He turned to Dan.

"It's more than generous. I didn't expect that much."

"No more than your mother deserves," Jacob said, his voice sounding husky with emotion. "I'm just sorry that it comes so late to her. As to your share for the children's program, I wanted to add more than we'd initially discussed. By creating an annuity for your City Kids, you'll be able to operate freely for a longer period of time. I expect it will become self-perpetuating.''

Dan was moved. ''Thank you for thinking of that. I wouldn't have.''

Jacob nodded, looking satisfied. ''Does anyone have any objections or problems with the draft?''

His advisors closed their notebooks and the gaunt, gray-haired one cleared his throat. ''*Nein,* Your Highness.''

''Then print it up in final form, will you, Wilhelm? We'll get on with plans for the ball.''

Dan sat with Jacob through the remaining meetings of the day at the king's invitation, although he felt of little use. Still, it seemed to be something Jacob wanted him to do—as if he was trying to include Dan in this official part of his life to make up for their earlier quarrels. As he heard Jacob negotiate with his cabinet, then his household staff, and finally with his social secretaries each element of the next few weeks' activities, he found himself more and more amazed by how hard Jacob worked and how sharply he focused on details. And through it all, Jacob listened attentively to suggestions and never dismissed anyone's ideas as without worth. He was a fair, generous and intelligent ruler, and Dan began to feel pride growing inside for this brother he'd never known he had.

As the night of the ball approached, excitement mounted in the castle. Elly felt it in the kitchens as Cook organized her army of assistants, some of them gifted chefs in their own right. A menu was designed and vast quantities of ingredients ordered. Supplies arrived daily and were added to the immense walk-in refrigeration units in the castle's cellar. Wines were delivered by the case. And as the day neared, the fresh vegetables and meats came by the truckload.

Then there were the candles, by the hundreds, placed in sconces high on the stone walls of the immense ballroom. Banners were brought out of storage and cleaned to be ready for hanging. Flags of the attending nations were mounted in long rows leading from the castle gate through the courtyard and up to the front entry. Tables seemed to sprout from nowhere and were positioned along with chairs below the raised dais where the royal family would be seated. Elly's heart raced with anticipation.

And every night, Dan came to her room. They lay together on her bed and discussed the day's events. They laughed at the antics of the little prince and princess, and admired Jacob and Allison for their grace in handling what could have become an endless battle with the paparazzi. But after the talk and laughter, they made long, delicious love.

The one thing they never discussed was the future, for it was still forbidden ground. Nothing that Elly could see had changed in Dan's desire to have a family or her need not to have one. Although she thought about offering to adopt a baby with him, she sensed that this would be a terrible disappointment to a man who was capable of producing his own children. At times she felt so inadequate that she cried silently into her pillow after he had fallen asleep. When all was said and done, she knew that if the brothers' plan worked it would mean the end of her relationship with Dan. For leaving Elbia would mean losing Dan to his future bride, the mother of his children, whoever she might be.

Eight

The night of the ball, the castle was ablaze with lights, and the delectable aromas of a hundred different foods wafted from the kitchens and through the halls. Dan and Elly had discussed the evening's escort arrangements. Elly had told Dan he should really accompany his mother and she would enter the grand ballroom on her father's arm.

"But I get the first waltz," he had insisted.

"Definitely…well, unless Tom shows up…" Her eyes twinkled mischievously.

"Cruise?"

"You got it."

He laughed at her. "Deal."

But when he left his room dressed in the tuxedo Jacob had lent him, since they were nearly identical in size, he turned down the hallway toward Madge's room and saw two figures leaving it.

"Hey there, you stealing my girl?" he shouted, laughing.

"Sure thing, what you gonna do about it?" Frank Anderson retorted. He grinned at Madge. "Doesn't this young man of yours have a date of his own?"

"I know we discussed going together, Danny," she said coyly. "But Frank thought it might be nice if you two children went as a couple, then we could..."

"I get the picture," Dan grumbled, as if disappointed, although he definitely was not. "This is a setup."

Frank shrugged. "You two seem to be spending a lot of time together." He gave Dan a long look, as if for the first time considering the younger man's intentions toward his daughter. "We thought you and Elly might appreciate making your entrance together, if only to stir up the press one last time."

Dan hesitated, feeling awkward. "I hope you don't have a problem with my seeing your daughter, sir. She's a wonderful woman, and I have only the best intentions toward her."

"No problem," Frank said gruffly. He offered his arm to Madge and she slipped her hand through the crook. "I just don't want to see Elly get hurt. You wouldn't do anything to harm her, I know. Would you, son?"

There was grit underlying the man's polite tone, and his pale eyes hardened for just an instant. Dan suspected Madge, who was preoccupied with arranging the folds of her gown, wasn't in a position to see them. But he read Anderson's look as a warning.

"I would never do anything to hurt Elly," Dan stated firmly, meeting her father's gaze. "Never."

Frank nodded and his smile returned, all signs of a

storm gone. "I was sure that was the case. Why don't you go fetch her now? She must be anxious to join the party."

"Yes, sir, I will." Dan stood in the middle of the long stone corridor and watched his mother and Frank walk away, chatting amicably. The excitement for the evening had left him. He felt a chill through his bones as he replayed Elly's father's words.

Frank hadn't threatened him by any stretch of imagination. What he'd done was merely place a sobering thought before him. Which was that, just by encouraging Elly's affections, he was laying the foundation for breaking her heart. Because they both knew that, as hard as she'd tried to deal with her fears, ultimately nothing had changed. Their relationship existed only on a day-to-day basis. No commitment to the future existed.

Feeling far less festive, Dan walked slowly along the guest wing and stopped in front of Elly's door. The same door he'd entered with his spirits joyfully sailing many nights before this one. Now the ship of his heart was dragging the bottom of a dark cove, and he had to haul himself up out of the depths of his depression to put on a smile when he knocked on Elly's door. He wouldn't say anything to her about his discussion with her father. That would only upset her, and he wanted the little time they had left together to be happy. He could at least give her sweet memories.

He knocked.

"Come on in, Dad!" she called through the door.

"It's not Dad," he responded, forcing cheer into his tone. He stepped inside. "The senior branches of our families have run off without us. We'll just have to—"

He broke off, stunned then mesmerized by the vision before him.

For the next two minutes, Dan felt incapable of speech. He barely breathed and nearly tripped over his own feet. Elly stood shimmering in the light from a tall antique bronze floor lamp. The pale green of her dress appeared as light as sea foam, and the gleam of her red hair, piled loosely on top of her head, might have been a flame for the fire it ignited in his loins. A gold choker clasped around her throat was centered by an outrageously large emerald.

"Lord but you're beautiful, woman."

She smiled. "That's the sort of reaction I like from a man. What were you saying?"

"Your father and my mother have run off to the ball together. I'm to escort you." He moved closer and gave her a playful leer. "Lucky me."

She ducked away from his reaching hands. "We don't have time for that now," she said, laughing.

"I just want to feel the fabric."

"Right."

"Honest."

"I think we'd better save all that feeling stuff for later. Jacob expects us downstairs for the receiving line at exactly eight o'clock, and it's— Oh my gosh, it's seven-forty-five now!"

Elly snatched a silk shawl from the back of a chair, gave her hair one final glance in the mirror, and whisked past Dan. He dove in front of her to swing the door open a fraction of a second ahead of her. Shutting it behind him, he quickly caught up with her to offer his arm.

"Slow down." He laughed and patted her hand where it rested on the ebony sleeve of his jacket.

"Nothing's going to happen until we get there. They won't even open the castle gates to guests until eight."

"I'm just worried about what will happen once the press arrives. You and Jacob seem so sure that everything will be fine, but isn't this like inviting foxes into the hen house?"

"You think they will find some way to use the ball to make things even worse for Jacob?"

"Or for you. Yes, it could happen. There always seems to be an angle they can manipulate to create the appearance of scandal."

Dan frowned. "I've wondered about that too. But we've come this far and there's no turning back with over five hundred guests about to fill the ballroom."

From the far end of the corridor, bright lights flickered and glowed, and an orchestra played. Elly drew a deep breath and entered the immense hall on Dan's arm. She knew she should have been praying that everything would work out that night as planned. Instead, she felt a deep sadness because, if all did go well, this night would mark the end of everything the two of them had shared. It was one thing to sleep with Dan for a few days or even weeks, secure in the knowledge that she couldn't become pregnant because they were being careful each and every time. It was another to remain in a long-term relationship that he might try to alter to meet his desire for a family. He was single-minded and stubborn enough a man to think he might succeed.

Elly's heart fluttered with emotion as they crossed the ballroom toward the royal couple of Elbia, bedecked in jewels and formal regalia. She tried to focus on the next few hours, which would be so important to all of them.

Jacob wore the legendary von Austerand crown, and Allison a diamond-and-sapphire necklace that set her eyes sparkling. But all Elly could think as she took step after step toward them was that the man at her own side, whose arm she now leaned on, the same man who had wrapped his arms around her in passion, would soon leave her. She almost wished the brothers' plan would fail, compelling Dan and her to stay shut up in the castle another week...a month...an eternity. But she knew that was foolishness. Nothing she could do would delay their inevitable parting.

Conversely, she had never felt as close to any man as she felt to Dan. Letting him go would be the most difficult and painful thing she'd ever done.

When they at last stopped in front of the royal couple, Elly curtsied to Allison and Dan made a real bow to his brother. "Looks like you have a good turnout," Dan commented to Jacob, keeping his voice low.

"Indeed." Jacob lifted one coal-black eyebrow. "The question now is, will they be satisfied with the show we have to offer them?"

Dan took his place in the receiving line to Jacob's left, and Elly stood beside Dan. She looked around the vast hall but couldn't find her father or Dan's mother among the guests slowly entering through the three sets of soaring doors at the far end. She hoped that Madge hadn't succumbed to last-minute jitters and decided not to come. On the other hand, her father could be very persuasive when he wanted to be. She would leave that worry to him.

"By the way," Jacob said, slanting a mysterious glance at his queen, "we've discovered the culprit who leaked news of our brotherhood to the press."

"You have?" Dan asked, suddenly alert.

Elly leaned forward to listen. Whoever it was, she was sure Jacob would fire him or her immediately for such a serious breach of trust.

"Yes," Allison said solemnly, although her eyes twinkled as if she were secretly amused. "It seems that Cray's fascination with telephones is to blame. Gretchen told me that she was changing the baby one day when the phone rang and Cray picked it up. She didn't think anything of it at the time, believing he was talking to me or Jacob."

"Apparently, the switchboard operator had meant to connect a reporter to our public relations office, but in error rang the nursery," Jacob explained. "Cray launched into one of his usual chummy conversations that encompass everything from what he had for breakfast to parroting things he's overheard his parents talking about."

Allison rolled her eyes in motherly exasperation. "Gretchen remembers him saying something about his daddy having a big brother in America. But by the time she took the phone from him the caller had hung up. Whoever it was, he must have rushed straight off to chase down more leads."

Elly laughed out loud. "Oh no!" She looked at Dan, who was shaking his head in amazement.

"True," Allison said. "I think we're going to have to monitor the young man's calls until he learns that gossiping to strangers is different from talking with family members."

A burst of motion erupted near the immense central doors, interrupting the group's shared amusement. A dozen photographers broke through a line of dignified couples who had been approaching the dais. They rushed across the ballroom, cameras clutched in front of them, brushing roughly between guests who stared with irritation at them. Elly looked on helplessly as Jacob's security team closed ranks in front of the receiving line.

"Nein!" Jacob said, his voice sharp. "Let them through."

"They can wait until the formal announcement," Dan suggested gruffly.

"No. We might as well let them take their shots."

Elly stood nervously at Dan's side as the paparazzi's cameras flashed and whirred, and some of them shouted questions at the king and his brother. Jacob answered in a controlled voice for both of them. "It's only fair that we wait until everyone is here, gentlemen and ladies of the press. If any questions aren't answered when I make my statement, you'll have time to ask then."

Dan stood stiffly and nodded his agreement.

Elly scanned the room and finally spotted her father leading Madge their way. She caught his eye and shook her head subtly, warning him off. She didn't want Madge to be caught in the barrage of camera-wielding reporters.

Then her gaze skipped to a newly arrived party—a famous Italian actress and her movie-producer husband, accompanied by an entourage of three other couples. One man she recognized as a British soccer champion, another an American actor who had just won an academy award. The women with them looked so familiar, she was certain she must have seen them in recent movies. An idea struck her.

"Oh!" she cried out excitedly, tugging on Dan's arm. "Isn't that Maria Stanza!"

In a single wave of motion the photographers swiveled in the direction Elly was pointing. A second later, the entire press corps was dashing across the room, dodging past less notable guests to reach their new quarry. Flashes exploded, questions were shouted, but they were all aimed at someone other than the royals.

Allison glanced down the line toward Elly and smiled appreciatively. Jacob's expression hadn't altered, but his vivid blue eyes appeared relieved.

"Very smooth," Dan commented in her ear, giving her a quick squeeze.

Elly grinned. It looked as if Miss Stanza was enjoying the attention, and her friends were getting some welcome publicity as well.

After the receiving line disbanded, the guests danced to an orchestra that alternated Viennese waltzes with classic love songs and modern tunes. The press was kept busy recording the images and words of distinguished politicians, sports figures, and entertainment industry stars. It was ten o'clock before Elly knew it, then the music stopped and Jacob stood on the dais to make his speech.

The crowd's chatter gradually hushed and everyone looked up at the young king.

Jacob welcomed everyone in German, then in French, and finally in English, which was the language in which he chose to make his statement:

"Ladies and gentleman, I thank you for your attendance," he said solemnly. "I intend to keep this very short. Most of the information you require for your articles is contained in the detailed press release that you are about to receive. It includes a complete history of my father's relationship with a lovely woman by the name of Margaret Eastwood, before his marriage to my mother. This relationship had been kept a secret by my father and Ms. Eastwood in order to protect all involved parties. My mother never knew of it, and neither did I until recently.''

Jacob drew a deep breath and looked around the silent room. ''It is with great pride that I welcome my brother Daniel Eastwood to our country. He has become a friend to me personally and to my family during his stay with us. We value him as a strong addition to our family.''

Hushed voices rose from the crowd as guests looked at one another in surprise. But Jacob didn't pause.

''Although Daniel has a right to claim the throne of Elbia as his own, being the older of my father's only two children, he has elected to pass that right to me. For that I am grateful, I wish to continue serving my people as their king. Daniel has in no way been forced to this decision, and has asked nothing for himself. But it is only fair that his mother be compensated for the years she spent raising my father's son, my brother, on her own. And I believe my brother himself should receive some benefit as well.''

Elly glanced at Dan. He seemed to be concentrating very hard on Jacob's words. She caught a worried look in his eyes.

''What's wrong?'' she whispered.

''He's changed the speech we agreed on. I'm not sure what he's up to.''

Elly felt a warning chill climb her spine. Would Jacob dare to double-cross Dan in some way? If so, before all of these people there would be little Dan could do about it.

Jacob continued. ''My brother is a man of pride and many talents, not the least of which is the talent to share with the less fortunate. He would have left Elbia with nothing for himself, with only a small grant for his favorite charity. But I have decided that that is not enough."

Dan's face flushed, and Elly was sure he was about to protest, but a quick devilish smile from Jacob seemed to confuse him long enough to make him hesitate and say nothing for the moment.

"The crown has decided to give a sum of three million dollars to City Kids beach program in the form of an annuity in Daniel Eastwood's name. The interest earned by this annuity will enable the program to thrive independently of future donations. In effect, it will be self-perpetuating beyond the life of its founder."

Elly swallowed. She had never expected such a generous settlement, and when she turned to see Dan's reaction she could see how moved he was. The redness of his face had faded, but now he seemed in shock.

After the applause of the crowd died down, Jacob continued in a strong and calm voice. "There is, however, one more wrong that must be righted. An endowment of honor that cannot be ignored. I'm sure my father would have wanted to do this himself, if he were alive today...so it remains to me." Jacob's and Dan's eyes met. The first giving nothing away to the second. "My brother, though we did not share the same mother, might have been a king but for his fairness and generosity. If he is not to be king, he can be no less than a prince. Certainly not in my family's eyes. Therefore, I hereby endow Daniel Robert Eastwood with the honorary title of Prince of the Realm."

The room stood in stunned silence for two entire seconds, then broke into applause and shouts of "Long live Prince Daniel!" Champagne circulated on trays around the room, music played and guests laughed and shouted in approval. In the mayhem, Dan turned to Jacob.

"You couldn't leave well enough alone, could you?" he grumbled.

"It wouldn't have been right, *mein Bruder,*" Jacob said.

Dan nodded. "You know, I'll never live this prince thing down back on the streets of Baltimore."

"I expect not." Jacob smiled. "All the more pleasure for me to have given you the title."

"Some brother you are."

"And you!" Jacob responded, slapping him soundly on the back.

The night was a dazzling success after that. An hour later, most of the press suddenly departed, rushing to file their stories with their papers and magazines, hoping to get a jump on their rivals. Although they might rearrange facts to spice up their stories, Jacob and his advisors seemed satisfied that the final outcome would be relatively tame. Besides, there had been bigger game afoot in the form of the celebrities they'd photographed and interviewed. With only so much space in each publication, it seemed a sure thing that Maria Stanza's rumored affair with her chauffeur would attract far more attention than Jacob's peaceful welcome of his brother.

The evening flew past in a whirl of color, music and laughter once the paparazzi had departed. The guests began to relax and enjoy one another's company. Old friendships were renewed; new ones begun. Although English was spoken by nearly everyone and Elly was comfortable speaking with people from all over Europe, there were snatches of a dozen other languages to be heard among the guests. Laughter and dance were the universal languages, though, and she found herself to be a popular partner. For nearly two hours she danced every dance with some of the most charming men of all ages she could ever hope to meet.

But not one of them made her heart sing as it did when Dan's eyes met hers across the vast, crystal chandeliered room and his hand rose toward her at the first strains of the Blue Danube waltz, inviting her to join him. They met in the middle of ballroom, and he lifted her right hand delicately in his left, placed his right palm at the small of her back, and smiled down at her.

Her heart melted as they circled the room. Suddenly, it seemed the hundreds of guests around them simply evaporated into the air, and she was floating, the soles of her satin slippers barely whisking across floor. The pale green silk of her gown swooshed around her ankles. His wide tuxedoed shoulders leaned into each turn as they spun. Ceiling-high mirrors flashed past them. Marble walls seemed to dissolve into sugary-white clouds. It was a night for fantasies, a night when nothing could go wrong.

"You're not a bad dancer, Mr. Eastwood," she teased. "For a swimmer, that is."

"You're no stumbling Jane yourself." His dark eyes studied her approvingly, then he gave her a sexy smile. "For a nosy little bookworm, that is."

She pouted at him. "Does that mean I'm forgiven for intruding on your peaceful beach-town existence?"

"Forgiven totally," he murmured. "And then some."

She felt herself blushing at the intensity of his gaze as they whirled to the romantic strains of the violins. "What does that mean?"

"I'll be eternally grateful to you for bringing me and

Jacob together. He's a great man, and I expect we will become close friends over the years."

"I'm glad everything has worked out between the two of you." And she meant it wholeheartedly.

"There's more," he said, his voice lowering solemnly. "I'm thankful I've had the chance to know you, Elly. We're very different people, and learning about each other hasn't been easy at times. But I'll never forget the special moments we've shared."

"Like this one?" she whispered, her voice trembling.

"Like this one. Yes." Then he held her closer, and they spun faster and faster until she was laughing from the sheer joy of being held in his arms and being part of these precious seconds in both of their lives.

It was after two a.m. when Elly walked to her room by herself, thinking about the night. She had left while Dan was still busy talking to Jacob because she wanted time to herself.

This is it, she thought. The end of a romance that had been fated to last no longer than a brief affair. There remained no reason for her to linger in Elbia. She didn't need her father's reminders during the evening that they had other jobs waiting for them at home. Jobs that had been hastily put aside until the missing von Austerand heir could be found. Well, now he had been found, and there was nothing more for her to do here…or in Ocean City to which Dan would be returning.

"Elly."

She turned at the sound of her name echoing through the long passageway, and her heart swelled. She couldn't look at Dan, though. Her eyes fell to the stone floor, filling with tears. *Oh, damn,* she thought.

"What's wrong?" he asked, striding quickly along the corridor to join her. "The evening went very well, I thought."

"I'm happy that you and Jacob have reconciled your differences. Now it should be safe for you and your mother to return home."

"Then why the tears? It's us, isn't it?"

She nodded. "I should…*we* should never have gotten involved, knowing how different we are. Now it will be a hundred times harder to say good bye."

"Do we really have to say good bye?" he asked, tenderly touching a wide finger to her damp cheek. His eyes were too gentle, too full of emotion for her to meet them for more than a second.

"Yes," she said bravely. "We do. And you know why, so please don't ask for another round of explanations."

"You're everything I've ever wanted in a woman," he said forcefully.

"Everything except one."

"You might change your mind. With time."

She shook her head. "No. I've always known I would never have babies. It's part of who I am—this too-big heart. Just like my mother's." She gazed tearfully up at him. "I love kids, though, and if you ever consider adopting…well, maybe—"

The look on his face stopped the words that clogged up in her throat.

"I realize there are kids without parents and homes." He was angry now. She could hear it in his tone, which chilled her. "I try to help a lot of those kids, in my own way. But I want my own children too. Adoption isn't for me.''

She searched frantically for an area of compromise. ''Maybe a surrogate mother. Your genes would still—''

''Are you crazy, Elly?'' He seized her by the shoulders and shook her hard. ''Why would I want to impregnate another woman when I have you?''

She shrunk from his grasp. ''You don't *have* me. That's just it,'' she whispered hoarsely. ''Not if you intend to use me to produce your progeny like a living test tube.'' She ducked away from him when he tried to reach for her again.

''Elly, we can't just throw away these last few weeks. We've shared too much.''

''I'm not throwing them away!'' she shouted through her tears. ''I just want you to leave me alone. I can't do it! Don't you understand? I just can't do it, Dan!''

Sobbing, she broke for her door, shouldered it open then ran into her room. She didn't remember hearing the door close but it did, with the dull thud of finality a moment after she hit the bed at a run. Burying her face in a pillow, she wept bitterly. Mourning the loss of the only man she'd ever truly loved, mourning the loss of the children she might have had, if she'd had a normal heart and been strong enough, brave enough.

For a long time, she thought she was alone in the room, then she felt the bed ease down under the weight of someone sitting beside her.

''Don't say it,'' she choked out over the tears. ''It won't make any difference.''

''Say what?''

Had she guessed wrong? If so she was about to make a worse fool of herself. "Don't say that you love me."

"All right. I won't say it. And you needn't say it either."

"Yes," she said. "It's better that way."

He took a deep breath. "Will you at least take some time to think about your decision?"

"I've had plenty of time—years. Nothing has changed or ever will."

"Come with me to Maryland," Dan begged. "We can talk more."

She shook her head, fraught with pain. "There's no use prolonging the inevitable. It will be easier if I put you...put *us* behind me."

Dan wrapped his arms around her. "I promise, Elly. I won't let anything bad happen to you."

She pushed him away and glared into his eyes. "And you think my father wanted something *bad* to happen to my mother? He couldn't protect her when her heart gave out. How do you propose to protect me?"

He looked down at his hands in desperation. They both knew the answer. The only way he could shield her from her worst fear was by swearing they would never have a child together, and that was something he was unwilling to do. He'd never give up. He'd argue them both to exhaustion.

Her heart felt heavy in her chest, and hot, and her breaths came in shallow tugs as she took in the look of disappointment on his face. Even so, it couldn't outweigh her own regrets.

"So, this is the way we say our farewells?" he asked.

She reached out and touched his cheek, then laid her palm along the strong line of his jaw. "I'd rather say goodbye in a different way, if you still have—'' Her eyes strayed to the bedside table drawer. ''That is, if you still want to.''

He nodded soberly. ''I couldn't let you go any other way, Elly.''

And she let him take her in his arms, believing beyond doubt that he would keep his word and hold her safe this one last time before they parted forever.

His gentleness moved her. Wherever Dan touched her, he touched with reverence and, although he never said the words, love was written in every caress, in every kiss, in every movement of his body over hers.

As Elly kissed him, she told herself over and over again, This is the last time I will ever feel this man's body next to mine, his weight on me, his power within me.

She cherished every second, branded her mind with each passionate touch of his hands, his lips. He slid his chest down over her breasts, and she closed her eyes and concentrated on the lovely rough texture of the curled hairs over the sensitive flesh of her nipples.

The heaviness and firm promise of his masculinity pressed against her thighs, and she gently lifted one leg to nudge him. Dan moaned softly, gripped her hand and guided it downward then wrapped her fingers around himself. She stroked him, memorizing the contours that mimicked velvet-over-fist hardness, and she ached to feel him inside her.

Still lower he moved until his lips grazed her breast, then teased first one then the other dark saucer of nipple to a tight, hard peak between the sharp edges of his teeth. She pressed herself upward against his mouth, wanting to remember even the muted twinges of pain along with the seething pleasure.

Elly gripped him harder, even as his hand slid between her thighs and found her warm center. Although she had been ready and eager for him from the moment he joined her on the bed, and he must have sensed as much, he slowly caressed her, at first with only the very tips of his fingers, then with more urgency, moving the length of his long fingers within her. Her eyes shot wide open as flames rushed through her and she clung to him, unsure she could survive another second yet greedy for more. Wave after wave of delicious heat seized her and she writhed with pleasure and called out his name, begging him not to stop. Ever. Ever.

Then his hands parted her thighs and she eagerly took him into her, savoring, dying with the fullness of him as he slid in and out of her, hitting all the most deliciously sensitive spots with each passage, driving her mad with ecstasy. And she knew there would never be another man like this one. Dan. Who had touched her so deeply but would soon leave her. So that when he at last thrust himself fully deep into her, filling her, completing her, and she knew from the iron tension of every muscle in his body that he was nearing the final moments before his own climax, she held on and wouldn't let herself release wholly until she could no longer control the crescendo of her passion. Then she gave herself over utterly to him, and they soared together, each one nourished by the other's rapture.

Dan reluctantly left Elly's bed, just long enough to dispose of the protection he'd worn. His body felt satisfyingly spent, but his heart was in shreds. Even as he'd made love to her, he'd been in agony. The knowledge that this was the end of all they'd been to each other, rather than the beginning of a long and happy life together, tore him apart. And so he wasn't thinking about what he was doing as he removed the condom, but something felt strange, and it occurred to him that he should pay attention. He thought he could feel the pad of his own finger against his thumb, where latex should have been.

He looked down.

It wasn't a large tear, but it was badly placed, near the tip of the sheath, and it seemed certain that the opening was large enough to have leaked. A hollow, gritty feeling settled in his stomach, and he felt a sudden lurch of desperation before he reminded himself of how slim the odds were that anything could have happened as a result of one unprotected incident.

He looked back through the open bathroom doorway to the bed where Elly lay, entwined in white sheets, her eyes closed, a sweet smile on her lips. He should tell her. But was there really any point in frightening her for no reason? This had been their last time, and it should be perfect for her. She was leaving him, and all he wanted was to let their good byes this night be as sweet as possible.

Let it be, a voice from inside whispered. And so, he did.

Nine

Elly woke to find Dan still beside her in the bed. For a moment, her heart soared as she reached out to stroke the fine, dark hairs in front of his ear. She rested her chin on the firm muscles of his shoulder and pressed her lips lightly to the side of his neck, now sexily rough with new whiskers.

She would miss this intimacy…miss Dan in any setting or context more than she could say. But it was clear he needed the family he had dreamt of for so long, and she was only in the way. There had never been any getting around that.

The tightness in her chest grew to a suffocating ache. Tears filled her eyes, blurring her vision of his long, strong body tangled in the sheets. She slowly lifted her hand away from his face and turned away to roll out of bed. The ache turned to a crushing pain that made it nearly impossible for her to straighten up or breathe as she walked into the bathroom. Grabbing blindly at a strip of toilet paper she dabbed at her eyes and choked back sobs, wishing for strength.

Leaving Dan...oh, how was she ever going to do it!

Furious with herself for breaking down, Elly tossed the soggy tissue at the little wastebasket beside the toilet and missed. She bent to scoop it up and, this time from a squat, placed it there, her eyes focusing hazily on a filmy object beside her tear-damp tissue.

Something was wrong.

She couldn't have said what, at first. The condom was an amorphous shape, just a lump really. But it suddenly appeared to her to have *two* open ends, which was, of course, impossible. She lifted it gingerly from the basket, thinking to prove her eyes were playing tricks on her. But when the thin layer of material lay in her palm, she could see a finger-width tear, and her heart felt as if it had stopped.

"No," she breathed. "Oh please, no."

Perhaps the thing had torn as Dan removed it? Yes, that must be it. If it had happened while they'd been making love and he'd realized the problem, he would have told her. She swallowed, staring down at her hand.

Or would he? What if it had torn and he'd known it then done nothing about it? He had been inside her when he'd climaxed. The condom would have been useless. Her stomach churned, and she pressed a hand to her abdomen, her head whirling.

Then a worse thought occurred to her, as if there could be anything worse than carrying the seed of her own demise within her. What if Dan had intentionally sabotaged his own protection?

He had often said that he was sure she'd adjust to

motherhood if she only let herself stop worrying. Might he have decided to impregnate her, believing she'd then be forced to accept her condition and have his baby?

If he had tricked her or intentionally deceived her, she could never forgive him. If his crime had been less, and he simply hadn't realized until he'd removed the condom that anything was wrong, he was still at fault. She had a right to know.

Elly dropped the useless thing back into the basket and slowly stood up. She felt dizzy, and the space behind her eyes burned hot with anger then ice-cold from terror. So many emotions boiled within her she didn't know if she'd be able to speak.

Hold on, she cautioned herself. *First, find out how much he knows.* At the very least he must have seen the hole, for he couldn't have removed it without noticing.

She walked stiffly back into the bedchamber, took her robe from the bedpost, slipped her arms into it and tied it tightly around her waist.

Dan rolled over and smiled at her. It took him a moment to realize that Elly was not smiling back. In fact, she looked downright grim, worse than grim...close to exploding. "What?" he asked.

"I want to know what happened last night," she said evenly, though he thought he heard the beginnings of tears behind her words.

He slid up in the bed, pushed a pillow behind his head and tested one of his best boyish grins on her. "I had hoped you would remember. My ego is shattered."

"Damn your ego, Daniel Eastwood!" she spat. "Tell me when it happened—before, during or after we made love."

His heart felt as if she was gripping it in her cold

little hand, and squeezing the life out of it. "What do you mean, *before?*"

"Then you know about the hole. Did you intentionally tear the condom we used last night?"

He was shocked. "Of course, I didn't. Why would I—" But the condemnation in her eyes said it all. "You seriously believe I would try to impregnate you against your will?"

"I don't know—you seem to want that family of yours awfully badly. How far would you go to have things your way?"

"Not that far. Never!" he roared, tossing back the bedcovers. "And I resent your implying—"

"I'm not implying anything," she interrupted, her voice snapping like a tempest-tossed arctic wave. "I'm accusing you straight out, Daniel."

"Well, you're wrong. I would never intentionally hurt you or force you to do anything you didn't want to do." He found his briefs on the floor and pulled them on. How could she even think...? Well, he had kept the truth from her, so he supposed she might assume the worst. "I didn't realize it was damaged until it was too late."

"And when was too late? Before or after you climaxed inside me?"

He held back his rage as best he could, but his face felt on fire and his fists clenched spastically at his sides. He wanted to hit something. Not *her,* but something. To break things and watch them splinter. To work out his fury in a physical way, because, damn it to hell, words certainly weren't getting through to her.

"It was too late *after* we'd made love and I was disposing of the condom!" he roared.

She blinked at him suspiciously. "You didn't realize it was torn until then?"

"No. Don't you think I would have stopped?"

"I don't know. Would you have?"

"Yes!" he bellowed without hesitation. He stepped toward her, but she backed away, suddenly looking frightened. "Listen, there was nothing I could do about it last night. Telling you then would only have upset you and—"

"And you don't think I'm upset now?"

He shook his head, at a loss for what to say to her. He was making a worse mess of this, but she wasn't making things any easier on him. "I don't think it's as bad as you might believe. The odds are so small. Where are you in your cycle?"

"Near the end," she admitted. "My period should start in just a few days."

"There. It's even better than I thought." He was trying to speak in a calming tone, but he still wanted to shout at her that she was panicking for no reason. "Let's not spoil last night by fighting."

She sighed, gnawed at her bottom lip and looked away from him. A tear slipped from beneath her eyelashes. "I just wish it didn't have to end this way."

He moved cautiously toward her. "It doesn't have to."

She squeezed her eyes shut and shook her head, looking miserable. "It does. It really does. I couldn't stand wondering if whatever we chose for protection on any given night had worked. Nothing is foolproof. Last night should be enough evidence of that."

"No guarantees," he murmured, his heart aching. "Not in any part of life." Of course he'd always known that. But now he couldn't even imagine the family he'd once hoped for. Because no woman other than Elly would ever feel right to him as the mother of his children.

Elly lifted a shoulder in silent agreement. No guarantees.

"How soon will you leave Elbia?" he asked.

"As soon as possible. Work is waiting for me back home. I expect my father will stay to finalize the job here."

"Let me know when you have made plans for your flight," he said woodenly. "I'll want to see you off."

She didn't answer. And two days later when she stepped into the helicopter on the pad behind the palace, there was only her father to see her off because she wanted it that way. She couldn't have survived a farewell scene with Dan. She barely survived the flight home as it was.

Elly waited one week before working up enough nerve to take the test. For all that time she argued against her instincts. Dan was right; the odds were that nothing at all had happened and she was letting her imagination run away with her. But she had to know.

On her first attempt, she was so nervous she dropped the paper strip in the toilet bowl, invalidating the test. On her second try, her hand was shaking so badly she nearly dropped it again. Somehow she managed to hold onto the test strip long enough to get a reading. Then she dropped it because it was positive.

Her entire body trembled as if she'd been plunged into a winter sea. Her stomach lurched, spasmed, then tightened into a knot so hard she had to grab for the edge of the sink and gasp for breath. She forced herself to do a third test, just to be sure. It turned out the same way.

She was pregnant.

Elly didn't want this. This wasn't how her life was supposed to turn out. She had been perfectly happy without children. After all, some women weren't meant to be mothers. And she was one of them. If her mother had been satisfied having one child, she would most probably have lived a long life.

But if your mother had made the same choice that you made before you met Dan, a voice murmured in her ear, *you would never have been born.*

Elly sank to the bathroom floor and sat staring at the test slip.

A life. That was what this was all about. There was a life inside her, just as, at one time, she had been a tiny life inside her own mother. Her mother had cherished her and brought her into the world.

What would she do with this life Dan had given her? What could she do? She dropped her face into her hands and wept.

Dan returned to Ocean City with a sense that his world had been turned upside down, soundly shaken until all the reliable habits had clinked out like loose change to the ground, then stood back on its feet to face a totally new and foreign landscape. He no longer knew how to function.

While in Elbia, he'd longed to return to the Haven, to his turf, to daily swims up the shore and to his plans for City Kids. But figuring in all his dreams, he now realized, had been Elly. Standing on the beach and handing him a towel as her eyes grew huge when he strode out of the water. Walking around inside his

house, as relaxed and at home as she'd been with him
in Elbia. Curled up in his arms in his bed. She was
always there, in his mind and in his heart.

But no longer in reality.

The first week he was home, he concentrated on
work—contacting his banker to arrange for the trust
department to manage the royal annuity, putting his
Realtor to work hunting up additional property to add
to the Haven for his City Kids camp, bringing Kevin
up to date on the many changes that would have to be
made.

They were going to need a larger, full-time staff,
including camp counselors, and they'd add a cafeteria
and cook with helpers. These were all things that would
have wildly excited him at any other time. But they
seemed empty gestures without Elly.

Then there were Jacob, Allison and their two precious children. He had a brother now, a sister-in-law,
and he was an uncle! He was so very proud of Jacob
and all he'd done for his little country. Jacob had been
generous to him, personally, but had also helped so
many unfortunate people outside the family through the
royal charities.

Aside from all that, he envied Jacob. Not for his vast
wealth or for the power of his title. He envied his
brother for the love his family bestowed on him daily,
without reserve. And he wished with all his soul that
Elly had been able to give him that kind of unlimited
love...for he had believed he was capable of loving
her, if only she would let him.

At the end of a week, his pain and disappointment
had gnawed a hole through his heart so immense that
he no longer feared her rejection. He had to talk to her,

had to hear her voice even if all she did was send him away again.

He found the business card she'd given him on the day they'd met and punched in the long-distance number for Anderson Genealogical Research. An answering machine picked up, Frank's gravelly voice: "Your call is very important to us. Please leave your name, time of call and phone number so that we can—"

Dan hung up. His brow was sweating and his hand shook as he set the receiver down. An hour later, he tried once more. Again there was the machine. The following day, he called three times. And the next day three more times. Finally, he left a message: "It's me, Elly. Call. We have to talk." But four days later Elly hadn't called him back.

He was desperate, fuming and raw from her silent rebuffs. She had obviously put their affair behind her, but he could not forget. Slowly the thought came to him. A family was what he'd always wanted, yes. But if it came to choosing between having Elly and having babies with another woman, he knew of only one answer.

It must be Elly.

Perhaps it was too late, but perhaps not. He picked up the phone to make one last call. Long distance, to Elbia.

Jacob seemed happy to hear from him. "So have you already begun construction of your additions?" he teased, knowing how excited Dan had been to start work on his new project.

"Let's just say the ball is rolling but it has a long way to go. The reason I called was to see if Frank Anderson is still there. I've been trying to reach him through his office, but all I get is a machine."

"He's here," Jacob said. "I can have him call you."

"Good," Dan said. "I have to ask him for a favor."

"Oh? You need some additional research on your family?"

"No, I need to ask for his daughter's hand in marriage."

He could hear Jacob half choking, half laughing at the other end of the line. "You see," Jacob sputtered, "I knew something was up between you two. I wish you all the happiness."

"Wish me luck first. I'm not at all sure Frank will be happy about this. And Elly will need some high-power convincing."

"Then, good luck. And if there's anything I can do to help—"

"I'll call," Dan finished for him. But he knew, in his heart, that everything rested on him alone.

Later that day, Frank called, and it was clear that Jacob had prepared him for Dan's question. Dan had been justified in his concern. The man sounded none too pleased with Dan's intentions. "Of course I would give my blessing to anyone who loved Elly, and whom she loved as well," he muttered sternly. "I could see she had a certain affection for you. But it's my understanding that she has chosen not to pursue the relationship."

"Because of her mother," Dan said as gently as he could while still getting straight to the point. "Not because of anything that happened between us. She fears childbirth and knows I've always wanted children."

For what seemed a long time, Frank didn't respond. Dan wondered if he'd lost the connection, but before he could ask if Elly's father was still on the line, the older man began to speak in a low, troubled voice. "There's something you should know, if she hasn't already told you. Elly can never have kids of her own."

Dan frowned into the receiver. Something in the way Frank had phrased that last sentence made him suspicious. "Was that her decision or yours?"

"It's mutual," Frank snapped. "When we found out she had the same heart defect as her mother, we had a serious talk, she and I."

Dan winced, almost sure he could guess what was coming. "And you told her that you couldn't bear losing her the way you had lost her mother, is that it?"

"More or less. But it wasn't just what I wanted. She had been traumatized by her mother's death. And medically, it just didn't make sense for her ever to take the same risk, knowing what we knew."

Dan wondered how much pressure Frank had intentionally or unintentionally put on his daughter to remain childless. First by neglecting her when she'd most needed his comfort and support. Then, after he'd assuaged his grief, by drumming into her how much like her mother she was.

"I love my daughter and don't want to lose her," Frank continued defensively. "There's nothing wrong with that."

"And I love your daughter and I don't want to lose her either. So I'm willing to put aside my dream of a family to be with her." Dan paused, feeling angry and frustrated. "Is that all right with you, or have you also told her she shouldn't marry under any circumstances?"

"Taking that risk is up to her," Frank said coldly.

So that was it. All of her young life, her father had warned her about the dangers of men, marriage and having babies. And she had the death of her mother to prove him right.

"Someday you'll have to let her go, Frank. She's a grown woman now, not yours to keep. If she doesn't come to be with me, it will be with another man who won't love her as much or take as good care of her as I will."

The silence was worse than almost anything the man could have said. Dan guessed the man's blessing would not be forthcoming.

"Frank, at least talk to her for me. Ask her to return my calls, or I'll have to do this my own way. She'll resent your holding her back once she makes up her mind to live her own life."

"I know you mean well," Frank choked out. "I feel badly that I wasn't there for her when she needed me. But I'm here now and I will support whatever she wants. If that's to remain childless, that's what it will be, though." He hesitated. "I've been talking to your mother, and she says you're dead set to have kids. I expect that's what sent Elly heading for the hills."

"It probably is. But will you just put in a word for me? Encourage her to let me come up to Connecticut and talk to her."

"I'll do what I can," Frank promised.

"Whatever she says, I'll honor," Dan agreed. "All I'm asking for is one last chance."

Elly paced the floor, furious with her father. First he'd come home and, instead of pitching in with all the work that had to be done, he was off sightseeing with Madge, who had appeared at the airport on his arm, to Elly's shock. Then he'd taken Elly aside to tell her what a good man Dan Eastwood was. And it was clear that either Dan, his mother or both of them had gotten to her father, big-time.

She hadn't even been able to decide yet what she would do about the baby she carried. If the little life growing inside her could have been donated, like a spare kidney, to a woman who desperately wanted a child, she might have done it in the first few days after she'd discovered she was pregnant. But by the time she'd known for two weeks, she'd begun to wonder what this very new person inside of her would grow up to look like. And that had been her downfall.

Would he or she have Dan's dark hair, or her own red? Would their baby have his tall, strong build, or her more delicate bone structure? If she gave the child away, she would never know. And to give the child away, she'd have first to give birth to it, which was the reason she hadn't wanted to get pregnant in the first place.

Why couldn't life be easy!

She swung around at the sound of a car door slamming in her driveway. The Anderson Genealogy offices were located in the bottom floor of the house she shared with her father. She was upstairs in her bedroom and, when she looked out the window, a car with rental plates was sitting in the driveway. Dammit, it was *him*.

Elly raced downstairs, finger-combing her hair as she went, despite her intention not to let Dan in the house. She ran her tongue over her lips and tried to recall if she had put on makeup that day, then told herself to knock it off because she didn't care what she looked like when all she was going to say to Daniel Eastwood was, ''Sorry you made this long trip. I don't want to talk to you. Good bye.''

The doorbell rang. She stopped dead in the middle

of the office, unable to move a step closer to the door. He knocked on the door. She touched a hand to her chest and tried to breathe deeply, slowly, like a sane person. He pounded on the door. She began hyperventilating.

"Elly! I know you're in there. I ran into your father at the end of the street and he said so. Open up!"

No! she voiced the word, but nothing came out.

"I'm not going to stand out here forever, and I'm not turning around to go back to Maryland without having my say. Now open up or I'll let myself in the hard way."

She looked down at her hands. They were shaking so hard they looked blurry. "Coming," she whispered hoarsely.

She twisted the lock button in the middle of the knob and opened the door. Stepping back, she bowed her head so she wouldn't have to look at Dan as he moved past her into the room.

She sensed that he had stopped in front of her and, when she lifted her gaze by a few inches, there were the toes of his shoes facing her bare feet. "Say what you have to say," she said quietly, still not daring to meet his eyes.

He reached out and drew her roughly into his arms. "Elly, you're more important to me than anything in this world. Anything."

She buried her face in his chest and breathed in the scent of him. "You're saying that you've given up your dream of a family?"

"No, I'm ready to consider two a family. You and me. That's all I need to be happy. I love you, Elly, and I know you love me. That's got to be enough for us."

He sounded desperate and angry and determined...and she loved him for all those reasons.

But he didn't know yet what she knew. And she would have to tell him. "I can't...can't marry you until..."

"Until what?"

Until I decide if I'll keep your child or— No, she couldn't do that. She would never be able to reject Dan's baby. Which left only one alternative. To let it grow and thrive in her and not give it up. And for the first time it struck her that this little life didn't seem at all an intrusion. It felt a part of her, something that was meant to be, that had always been fated to be brought into the world, against all odds, on the strength alone of one man's wish for a family. And strangely enough, she felt okay with that, to be part of a larger picture of life. Not to be, as she'd feared she'd become in marriage, the victim of a man's design to fulfill his role as populator of the planet. She would share in a miracle, and happily so.

She looked up at Dan for the first time. "I can't marry you until...until you ask me," she whispered.

He stared down at her, looking like the most befuddled male on the planet. "What?"

"You're talking all around the issue. You never really asked if I would marry you."

"Good grief." He lowered his head to touch foreheads with her. "All right, woman." He knelt before her on one knee and produced a small box from his coat pocket. "I came prepared."

"I see you did."

"Elly, I love you for being you, with all your beauty, your intelligence, your kindness and your fears. I want you in my life. Anything else isn't worth losing you over. Will you marry me?''

"I won't take away your dream of having children," she said slowly.

His face fell. "Oh, Elly...please don't say—"

"Because I think a family is that important to you, a real family. So yes, I will marry you, Daniel Eastwood."

He frowned up at her. "Not to spoil the happiest day of my life, but I don't understand your answer. Are you saying that you will marry me and try to have a baby with me despite your heart problem?"

"I won't have to try very hard." She spread her hand over her stomach.

His eyes widened. "No. You aren't. We—"

"—made a baby the last time we made love."

"Then why didn't you call and tell—" He broke off, understanding showing in his eyes. "You still didn't want it when you found out. You were considering not telling me."

"I was," she admitted, touching his face tenderly. "I'm sorry, but I was. And I thought about every possible way I could avoid motherhood, until I had to face it. Then I remembered how much my mother loved me and how often she told me I was her most precious gift. I suddenly knew that if my little brother had been born, he would have given her just as much joy. Of course she knew the risks, but she took them anyway. I suppose all of life is a risk, isn't it?"

"You're still scared, aren't you?" he asked, kissing her gently on the lips.

"Yes." She lifted her chin another notch. "But I'll do everything I need to do to protect the baby and myself. God willing, we'll have a healthy baby.''

He held her for a very long time before speaking again. "Would you have called and told me all this if I hadn't come up here?"

She pressed her cheek against his chest and thought for a moment. "I don't know. I think so. But I'm very happy you told me that you wanted me for myself, not as just a means to a family. It made the decision so much nicer."

Ten

Dan and Elly's wedding was in the spring, before Elly started to show too much. As Allison adored weddings and felt a special closeness to Elly and Dan, who had fallen in love in Elbia, Der Kristallenpalast was offered as the setting for their wedding, as it had been for many others of the king's and queen's family members and close friends before. And Daniel Eastwood, Prince of the Realm, was definitely considered family now.

Frank beamed with obvious pride as his daughter walked down the flower-strewn aisle of the castle's chapel at his side. But Dan thought he saw another emotion in the older man's eyes. Perhaps sadness at losing his only child? Or was it a lingering touch of the fear he had instilled in Elly all of those years?

It gave him an uneasy moment, but he quickly pushed all doubts aside at the happy smile on his beautiful bride's lips.

Kevin, his best man, nudged him in the ribs. "You lucky dog, you," he muttered under his breath.

"I know," Dan said. "How well I know."

He gazed out over the pews. In the very front row was his mother. She had never looked more contented. Already she was talking about her grandson, for they'd had a first sonogram and knew that Elly carried a boy baby. The two women had immediately begun picking out little blue baseball suits, rough-and-tumble teddy bears and other toys the child would be incapable of playing with for a good two years after his birth.

Everyone seemed pleased that they were marrying, but no one could have been happier than Dan himself.

Although their honeymoon might have been anywhere in the world, they chose to spend a week in Elbia, the most romantic place in the world, according to Elly. After they returned to Ocean City, they immediately began work on the City Kids project. Elly still did some genealogical research for her father, via the Internet, then sent him results by e-mail. She enjoyed the work, which helped him but also gave her something interesting to do while waiting for the birth of their son.

She wasn't without worry as her due date neared, but Dan was always there to reassure her. They had found the best obstetrician for their needs—a woman who specialized in difficult pregnancies. She had put Elly on a restricted activity schedule during the final two months, but allowed her a walk along the beach each morning while Dan swam.

As they woke up to each new day together, Dan thanked the powers that be for the chance he'd been given to keep Elly in his life, and to start a family too.

It was as much as he'd ever dreamed of having, and far more than he had believed he'd ever possess.

It was an ordinary morning three weeks before Elly was to enter the hospital for the C-section that had been carefully arranged to deliver their baby without undue stress on Elly's heart. Waking slowly, she lay blissfully in the warm bed, then looked down at her left hand. Her wedding ring felt strangely tight, and the flesh around it seemed puffy, swollen. She frowned, but was distracted by an unusually strong stirring within her womb. Elly smiled, pleased to feel the baby so active, and reached out for Dan.

He moved beneath her hand. "Hmmm?"

"Wake up," she whispered. "Your son is doing jumping jacks in here." She brought his hand over to her belly.

Dan immediately rolled over and grinned as he pressed his palm against the firm mound of his wife's stomach. "He certainly is. This kid will be ready for the Olympic swim team before he's three."

Elly laughed, then winced at a sudden sharp twinge low in her back followed by a tight sensation in her chest.

"What is it?" Dan asked, immediately concerned.

She laughed again. "Nothing. I must have just slept at a funny angle. My back hurt for a moment, but now it's gone."

"You're sure?" He looked worried.

"Of course, silly." She started to move out from under the sheet. "I'll just get up and stretch, and—oh my!"

"Elly!" Dan threw off the bed covers and leaped across the bed to catch her as she teetered forward, clutching her swollen stomach. "What's wrong?"

"I don't know…I…" She gasped for breath, then smothered a cry as another pain twisted her insides and left her dizzy and helpless. "Doctor Shelton said…said everything was fine. Three more weeks to go but—"

"But what?"

"These feel like—" she gasped again, unable to catch her breath now, droplets of sweat popping out on her brow "—these feel like…like—"

"Contractions?" Dan asked.

"Y-yes." She lowered herself back onto the bed with Dan's help. Tears trickled from her eyes. The pain was bad, and her heart was racing. She could breathe a little better now, seated, but only in shallow, rapid intakes. She stared across the room into the mirror over the dresser. Her features were puffy and pink, and suddenly it was no longer her own face looking back at her. It was her mother's face, the day before she'd died. And then Elly remembered how her mother's hands had swollen too, just like hers, so much so that she'd had to remove her rings that final day of her life. "Oh, please, no—" she wailed.

"Elly…Elly?" Dan cried, but his voice sounded distant and all she could concentrate on was her body's struggle to deliver a baby that wasn't supposed to come, not this way, not with her heart pulsing out of control and working so hard, not without the professional help she needed to bring this child into the world.

Desperately she tried to calm her heart, tried to think only of the things she must do to make sure Dan's son was born strong and healthy, no matter what might happen to her. She was terribly dizzy. The room became a blur. If she could just hold on long enough for the baby to be delivered, to draw its own first breath, then the rest she could accept.

Please let my baby live, she prayed. *Please don't take both of us from this wonderful man!*

She looked up into Dan's panic-stricken face, swimming hazily before her, and reached out to touch it. But her fingertips brushed air and fell to her side as a deep voice bellowed out in terror.

Dan grappled for the bedside phone, then was dialing 911, even as his roar of denial still echoed in the bedroom. This couldn't be happening, he thought desperately. Had Frank been right all along? Had he jeopardized Elly's life by encouraging her to keep their baby? But she had come to want it just as much as he, and now he wouldn't let history repeat itself. Dan refused to let fate take this woman from him.

The emergency operator spoke calmly, asking all the right questions.

"How soon will the ambulance get here?" Dan demanded, one hand pressed over Elly's stomach, as if he could physically hold her to this earth.

"They're on their way now, sir. Stay on the line with me. Tell me how she's doing."

He looked quickly at Elly. Her face had drained of all color. "She's unconscious."

"Is she still breathing, sir?"

He lowered his ear to her lips and felt a delicate wisp of breath. "Yes. But her heart...I don't know how much of this she can take. The baby was starting to come. Tell me what to do!" he shouted into the phone.

"Just wait there with her, sir. Watch for the ambulance."

He stared frantically at the clock, then at Elly. Seconds ticked past. He couldn't bear just sitting here while her life and the life of their baby rested in the balance. How many minutes did they have?

"Call the hospital," Dan barked. "Tell them we're on our way."

"But sir, the medics will be…" The woman's words drifted emptily away.

He had a bad feeling. What if it took them twenty minutes…thirty minutes or more to get there? How long did it take for a woman with an over-stressed heart or a baby deprived of oxygen to lose their lives? Ten minutes might be too long. And the Haven was just about that far from All Saints Hospital.

He dropped the receiver back into the cradle, spun around and scooped Elly's limp body up off the bed. "Hold on, darling," he whispered in her ear. "It's not going to happen that way again. I promise."

It seemed to Elly that she was in two bodies at the same time—her own and Dan's. Or perhaps not, maybe she had become part of everyone and everything that surrounded her. She could feel the awful pressure in her back and stomach, more intensely than ever, and her heart wasn't behaving well at all. But the pain felt somehow remote, as if someone else had taken the burden of it from her.

She wasn't looking down on herself, as people who experienced near-death moments often reported. She was everywhere, all at once: on their bed at home, being lifted in Dan's warm arms, watching the two of them from the perspective of the bungalow as he carried her at a run to his car. It was as if she became part of him at that moment. She could hear his heart thudding steadily, pounding with a fury within his chest through her cheek. And although her eyes were shut, she felt as if she was seeing through his eyes as he drove, and she knew where he was taking her, to the hospital.

Then they were driving very fast, and she could see the car as clearly as if she'd been standing on the street corner watching it flash past. A horn was blaring, like an off-key siren, and they were weaving through traffic, screeching around corners, running red lights.

And all the while Dan never stopped talking to her. "You're not going to leave me, Elly. I won't let you. You're mine and you're staying on this earth until it's your time. This baby is going to be born, and you need to stay here and be his mother. Do you hear me, darling? And your husband can't live without you, so don't you even think of giving up."

Even as the car squealed to a stop and he was throwing open the driver's door and racing around the outside to open her door and scoop her limp body up off the seat, he was shouting at her, claiming her, stealing her from death's ravenous jaws and dragging her back to the living.

A woman's voice said, "We'll take her now. It's all right, sir."

"I'm staying with her," Dan insisted.

But suddenly his arms were no longer supporting her, and the cool surface of a gurney came up beneath her. A nurse and orderly were wheeling her away, dashing through shining doors and running down a long polished corridor.

"No! I need to stay with her!" Dan shouted, but he sounded distant now and she wanted to beg them to let him be with her, but nothing came from her throat. She was desperate to see him, to tell him how much she loved him, for it might be her last chance.

There was a sharp jab in her arm and a moment later her eyes flew open. Suddenly, she was one person again: Elly. And the pain in her stomach became hers again, and more severe than ever. But Elly smiled up at the nurse and through trembling lips said, "Whatever you have to do, save my son." She grasped the woman's hand. "Do you hear me? Whatever it takes, give that man out there his little boy." And there was no longer any fear.

Dan glared at the formidable steel doors separating him from Elly. He paced the hall, glared, paced. When he could stand no more, he bolted through the right-hand door, but there was a woman the size of a Cadillac on the other side, and she thrust herself forward, backing him out of the trauma room before he could even get a glimpse of Elly.

"Now you just mind your manners," she said to him. "You can only get in the way in there, and you'll be wanting those doctors with your wife to keep all their attention on her."

"She needs me! What if she's—"

"What she needs is the kind of help they can give her," she assured him, her voice softening now that she had shoved him down into a chair and he didn't appear to be getting up again. "You did your job, Daddy. You got her here. I understand you broke the last record at Indy coming cross-town. Let them do what they can. I'll be back in a few minutes to tell you how she's doing. I promise."

He nodded but couldn't say a word of thanks. His throat was so dry he was unable to swallow, his eyes burned with tears he knew he'd never be able to shed. If he lost her now...

Dan dropped his head into his hands and prayed for all he was worth that the woman he loved would still be on this earth an hour from now. He didn't dare ask for another day.

The light was bright and joyous and beckoning. Elly knew it would be wonderful to see even before she opened her eyes, for she could feel its soothing warmth on her closed eyelids. Her heart was at rest, and her body felt as light as the air blowing softly around her. She had never been happier or more at peace.

"Elly?" a voice called to her. It was him. Dan.

She smiled to herself, remembering how he'd looked the last time she'd seen him. He had been so handsome, his dark eyes fixed on her intently, his hair still all mussed from sleep. Yet she would have spared him the pain she had seen etched in the lines around his strong mouth and across his forehead. Then she had looked up at him from the bed they'd moved her to, smiled and asked, "Have you seen your son yet?"

The man had broken down and wept as he clutched her to him.

"Elly, are you awake, darling?" he asked now.

Slowly she opened her eyes. Behind him was the sunny yellow hospital room bursting with flowers. The blooms had come from all around the world. The biggest arrangement of pale pink roses had arrived yesterday with a card embossed with the royal crest of Elbia. All the nurses had come to stare in amazement at it. There had been delicate orchids from her father and Madge. And dozens of bouquets from strangers in Hawaii, England, Canada and as far away as Australia, from well-wishers who had read about the Secret Prince and his bride's brush with death on the way to the hospital. The couple and their new baby were the toast of the tabloids now.

Dan bent down and kissed Elly softly on the lips. "The doctor says you can go home today." He was grinning, his brown eyes rich with happiness.

"Really?"

"Really. He says you're doing just fine. You do feel strong enough, don't you? We can insist you stay another day if you like."

"Oh no," she said quickly. "I want to go home."

"Good, the nursery supervisor says we have to take Dan Junior before he breaks through the bassinette."

She laughed, delighted with her two men. "He's kicking out the end of it?"

"He's a pretty big boy with a lot of energy. No wonder you had a tough time with him." His smile dimmed slightly. "Elly, I know at one time I went on about having a lot of kids. But I never want to come this close to losing you again. This is it for us. I've decided that three is plenty. And you already know I was happy to call two a family."

She touched the side of his face, shaved smooth for the first time in days. "I know, my love. I know. But the doctor says that what happened the other day wasn't related to my heart at all."

Dan squinted at her. "He's sure? What was it then?"

"The symptoms of an anxiety attack are almost identical to those of a coronary seizure. I guess when I saw that my hands and face were swelling up like my mother's had just before her heart attack, I believed the worst. My breathing all but shut down. I couldn't get enough oxygen, and that made me dizzy and, finally, I lost consciousness. Once I came out of it with the help of a mild tranquilizer, I could deliver the baby normally."

"All the same, you scared the hell out of me."

She stretched up to kiss him softly on the cheek. "Doc says it's possible I might never have another episode like that again, but if I do, there are simple medications I can take to control the symptoms, so that things don't get out of hand."

"That's wonderful."

"I think so, especially since I've been thinking I might want another baby."

He studied her with amazement for a long minute, then drew her into his arms. "Only if we get one hundred percent clearance from the experts. Even then, I think I'd move you into a room here from six months on, just to be on the safe side."

She laughed at him. "You fuss over me too much. I feel stronger than I've ever felt."

"Good thing too," a voice called from the doorway over a sudden explosive wail. "Because this little tiger is ready for a five-course meal and, if you don't provide it, there will be heaven to pay!"

Dan and Elly turned to see their son kicking up a storm in the arms of a petite nursery attendant. Elly laughed at the woman's amused expression. "I hear DJ is giving all of you fits down in the nursery."

"He's a joy," the woman said, smiling down at the baby as she handed him over to his father. "It's just that he gets ornery when he's hungry."

"Just like his daddy," Elly said, her heart melting as she watched the expression on Dan's face soften with love for his son as he cradled the tiny bundle in his strong arms.

"I never get ornery," he protested mildly, his attention fixed totally on the squirming, squalling baby. "Never," he whispered in the baby's tiny ear, then kissed the soft red fuzz on top of his little head.

DJ stopped crying and looked up into the man's face. Elly's heart soared at the picture they made together—father and son. Her husband and her son. Life was perfect.

The nurse smiled as she turned to leave. "I'll be back for him in twenty minutes."

"May we keep him here in the room with us?" Elly asked.

"You're sure you feel strong enough, Mrs. Eastwood?"

"For him, yes. Please?"

"Sure. I'll let them know in the nursery."

"You don't have to do this," Dan said. "You should get your rest while you can. We'll be leaving for home in a few hours."

"I want to," Elly said. "I've been waiting all my life for this, and I didn't even know it. Now that I have both of you here with me, I'm not letting either of you out of my sight."

"Bad news," he said, watching as Elly parted the bodice of her gown to prepare to nurse the baby, "one of us has to go to work and the other will eventually need to go to school."

She sighed. "Party pooper."

As Dan bent down to place his son in Elly's arms then watched him hungrily seek out her nipple, his heart swelled with love and gratitude. He hadn't stopped thanking whatever invisible force had allowed him to keep Elly and see his son born healthy. He expected it would be a long time before he was able to accept their presence in his life as routine.

Sitting on the bed beside them, he curled his arm around Elly's shoulders and kissed her lightly on the brow. She was beautiful, she was his, and she'd given him the most precious gift any woman could give a man. He wanted to hand her the world, but the Haven would have to do. That and all the love he could give her, both in his heart and in the bed they would again share as soon as she felt ready.

"I love you, Elly," he whispered, nearly overcome with emotion.

"And I, you," she said, turning her soft hazel eyes up to gaze at him happily.

Then he kissed her on the lips and she returned his kiss with an energy that made him suspect it wouldn't be long before she invited him to join her in the passion they'd discovered halfway around the world, in a magical place called Elbia.

*   *   *   *   *

*Silhouette presents an exciting
new continuity series:*

**When a royal family rolls out the red carpet
for love, power and deception, will their
lives change forever?**

The saga begins in April 2002 with:

The Princess Is Pregnant!

by Laurie Paige (SE #1459)

**May: THE PRINCESS AND THE DUKE by Allison Leigh
(SE #1465)**

**June: ROYAL PROTOCOL by Christine Flynn
(SE #1471)**

Be sure to catch all nine Crown and Glory stories: the first three appear in
Silhouette Special Edition, the next three continue in Silhouette Romance
and the saga concludes with three books in Silhouette Desire.

And be sure not to miss more royal stories,
from Silhouette Intimate Moments'

Romancing
the Crown,

running January through December.

This Mother's Day
Give Your Mom
 # A Royal Treat

Win a fabulous one-week vacation in
Puerto Rico for you and your mother at
the luxurious Inter-Continental San Juan
Resort & Casino. The prize includes round
trip airfare for two, breakfast daily and a
mother and daughter day of beauty
at the beachfront hotel's spa.

INTER·CONTINENTAL
San Juan
RESORT & CASINO

Here's all you have to do:

Tell us in 100 words or less how your
mother helped with the romance in your
life. It may be a story about your engagement,
wedding or those boyfriends when you were
a teenager or any other romantic advice
from your mother. The entry will be judged
based on its originality, emotionally
compelling nature and sincerity.
See official rules on following page.

Send your entry to:
Mother's Day Contest

In Canada

P.O. Box 637

Fort Erie, Ontario

L2A 5X3

In U.S.A.

P.O. Box 9076

3010 Walden Ave.

Buffalo, NY

14269-9076

Or enter online at www.eHarlequin.com

All entries must be postmarked by April 1, 2002.
Winner will be announced May 1, 2002. Contest open to
Canadian and U.S. residents who are 18 years of age and older.
No purchase necessary to enter. Void where prohibited.

PRROY

HARLEQUIN MOTHER'S DAY CONTEST 2216
OFFICIAL RULES
NO PURCHASE NECESSARY TO ENTER

Two ways to enter:

• **Via The Internet:** Log on to the Harlequin romance website (www.eHarlequin.com) anytime beginning 12:01 a.m. E.S.T., January 1, 2002 through 11:59 p.m. E.S.T., April 1, 2002 and follow the directions displayed on-line to enter your name, address (including zip code), e-mail address and in 100 words or fewer, describe how your mother helped with the romance in your life.

• **Via Mail:** Handprint (or type) on an 8 1/2" x 11" plain piece of paper, your name, address (including zip code) and e-mail address (if you have one), and in 100 words or fewer, describe how your mother helped with the romance in your life. Mail your entry via first-class mail to: Harlequin Mother's Day Contest 2216, (in the U.S.) P.O. Box 9076, Buffalo, NY 14269-9076; (in Canada) P.O. Box 637, Fort Erie, Ontario, Canada L2A 5X3.

For eligibility, entries must be submitted either through a completed Internet transmission or postmarked no later than 11:59 p.m. E.S.T., April 1, 2002 (mail-in entries must be received by April 9, 2002). Limit one entry per person, household address and e-mail address. On-line and/or mailed entries received from persons residing in geographic areas in which entry is not permissible will be disqualified.

Entries will be judged by a panel of judges, consisting of members of the Harlequin editorial, marketing and public relations staff using the following criteria:
• Originality - 50%
• Emotional Appeal - 25%
• Sincerity - 25%

In the event of a tie, duplicate prizes will be awarded. Decisions of the judges are final.

Prize: A 6-night/7-day stay for two at the Inter-Continental San Juan Resort & Casino, including round-trip coach air transportation from gateway airport nearest winner's home (approximate retail value: $4,000). Prize includes breakfast daily and a mother and daughter day of beauty at the beachfront hotel's spa. Prize consists of only those items listed as part of the prize. Prize is valued in U.S. currency.

All entries become the property of Torstar Corp. and will not be returned. No responsibility is assumed for lost, late, illegible, incomplete, inaccurate, non-delivered or misdirected mail or misdirected e-mail, for technical, hardware or software failures of any kind, lost or unavailable network connections, or failed, incomplete, garbled or delayed computer transmission or any human error which may occur in the receipt or processing of the entries in this Contest.

Contest open only to residents of the U.S. (except Colorado) and Canada, who are 18 years of age or older and is void wherever prohibited by law; all applicable laws and regulations apply. Any litigation within the Province of Quebec respecting the conduct or organization of a publicity contest may be submitted to the Régie des alcools, des courses et des jeux for a ruling. Any litigation respecting the awarding of a prize may be submitted to the Régie des alcools, des courses et des jeux only for the purpose of helping the parties reach a settlement. Employees and immediate family members of Torstar Corp. and D.L. Blair, Inc., their affiliates, subsidiaries and all other agencies, entities and persons connected with the use, marketing or conduct of this Contest are not eligible to enter. Taxes on prize are the sole responsibility of winner. Acceptance of any prize offered constitutes permission to use winner's name, photograph or other likeness for the purposes of advertising, trade and promotion on behalf of Torstar Corp., its affiliates and subsidiaries without further compensation to the winner, unless prohibited by law.

Winner will be determined no later than April 15, 2002 and be notified by mail. Winner will be required to sign and return an Affidavit of Eligibility form within 15 days after winner notification. Non-compliance within that time period may result in disqualification and an alternate winner may be selected. Winner of trip must execute a Release of Liability prior to ticketing and must possess required travel documents (e.g. Passport, photo ID) where applicable. Travel must be completed within 12 months of selection and is subject to traveling companion completing and returning a Release of Liability prior to travel; and hotel and flight accommodations availability. Certain restrictions and blackout dates may apply. No substitution of prize permitted by winner. Torstar Corp. and D.L. Blair, Inc., their parents, affiliates, and subsidiaries are not responsible for errors in printing or electronic presentation of Contest, or entries. In the event of printing or other errors which may result in unintended prize values or duplication of prizes, all affected entries shall be null and void. If for any reason the Internet portion of the Contest is not capable of running as planned, including infection by computer virus, bugs, tampering, unauthorized intervention, fraud, technical failures, or any other causes beyond the control of Torstar Corp. which corrupt or affect the administration, secrecy, fairness, integrity or proper conduct of the Contest, Torstar Corp. reserves the right, at its sole discretion, to disqualify any individual who tampers with the entry process and to cancel, terminate, modify or suspend the Contest or the Internet portion thereof. In the event the Internet portion must be terminated a notice will be posted on the website and all entries received prior to termination will be judged in accordance with these rules. In the event of a dispute regarding an on-line entry, the entry will be deemed submitted by the authorized holder of the e-mail account submitted at the time of entry. Authorized account holder is defined as the natural person who is assigned to an e-mail address by an Internet access provider, on-line service provider or other organization that is responsible for arranging e-mail address for the domain associated with the submitted e-mail address. Torstar Corp. and/or D.L. Blair Inc. assumes no responsibility for any computer injury or damage related to or resulting from accessing and/or downloading any sweepstakes material. Rules are subject to any requirements/limitations imposed by the FCC. Purchase or acceptance of a product offer does not improve your chances of winning.

For winner's name (available after May 1, 2002), send a self-addressed, stamped envelope to: Harlequin Mother's Day Contest Winners 2216, P.O. Box 4200 Blair, NE 68009-4200 or you may access the www.eHarlequin.com Web site through June 3, 2002.

Contest sponsored by Torstar Corp., P.O. Box 9042, Buffalo, NY 14269-9042.

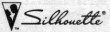

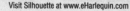